·JEANNE·
·UP·AND·DOWN·

Jane Claypool Miner

AN
APPLE
PAPERBACK

SCHOLASTIC INC.
New York Toronto London Auckland Sydney

ISBN 0-590-40053-3

12 11 10 9 8 7 6 5 4 3 2 1   7 8 9/8 0 1 2/9

Printed in the U.S.A.   01

First Scholastic printing, March 1987

·JEANNE·
·UP·AND·DOWN·

Look for these and other **Apple Paperbacks** in your local bookstores!

Chapter 1

"Three wishes?" Jeanne laughed and shook her head. "Why does it have to be three? Why not six, or fifteen, or three hundred?"

"Three wishes is all you ever get," her stepbrother Hank grumbled. "Anyway, three is plenty for most people."

"Tell me what the other ten people you interviewed wished for," Jeanne said. "Then I'll pick the best ones for myself."

"No, you have to come up with your own wishes." Hank held the clipboard away from his body as though he found the whole thing distasteful. "Think of something, and hurry. You're my last one and then I can go swimming."

"All right," Jeanne answered. "I wish I were thin. I wish I were blonde. I wish I were beautiful."

Hank wrote her answers on his clipboard and said, "Thanks, Jeanne. You're a good kid." Then, as he started toward the door, he stopped and grinned as he said, "You should have asked for something you had a shot at — like a million dollars."

"Go away!" Jeanne shouted and threw a pillow at him.

Hank ducked out the door and Jeanne tried to return to the novel she was reading, but her head was aching and her cold seemed worse. She turned fitfully in bed, plumping up the pillows and then blowing her nose for what seemed to be the thousandth time that day. Her thoughts were gloomy and she wished Hank hadn't forced her to admit how much she yearned to be different. She also wished she'd given him less personal wishes.

Though Hank hadn't seemed to take her response very seriously, it would have been easy to pass his questions off with a real joke. There was nothing funny about the answers she'd given him. She *would* give anything to be thin, to be blonde, to be beautiful.

She looked down at the photograph of the slender blonde heroine on the front of her book and smiled ruefully. While she might yearn to look like that, she would never be slender unless she stopped eating junk foods and went on a strict diet. But she would never, never be that beautiful because her face was just too different. There was no way you could turn a square jaw and high cheekbones into a perfect oval. Nor could a wide mouth and large teeth suddenly become a pretty little bow.

"You look down in the dumps." Her best friend Lori appeared in her doorway. "What are you thinking about?"

"Plastic surgery," Jeanne joked. She was so glad to see Lori that her mood changed completely.

Lori came over to sit in the chair beside the bed. She dumped a stack of books and a notebook on Jeanne's lap and continued, "No sense asking how you're feeling. You look miserable."

"Bored but better." Jeanne laughed and added, "That crazy Hank had this crazy assignment. I was thinking about my three wishes."

"He caught me at school today," Lori said.

"What did you wish for?"

"That David Green would look at me, that my father would stop yelling, and that I'd be the most famous actress in the world."

"Sensible wishes," Jeanne said. "I should have taken two out of three of yours."

"Your father never yells," Lori said. Then she narrowed her eyes in mock jealousy and hissed, "You'll never have him. David Green is mine, all mine."

"He's yours." Jeanne laughed. Lori had loved David since the first grade, but she'd never managed to have more than a two-minute conversation with him.

"If only he were yours to give," Lori said in a dramatic voice, with her hand placed over her heart.

"Ten years is a long time for unrequited love," Jeanne teased. "Maybe you should consider other options."

Lori shrugged, "If by other options you mean anyone else in the sophomore class, I'll stick with my dreams." Then she asked, "What did you wish for?"

"Plastic surgery?"

"No, what did you *really* wish for?"

"I wished to be thin, blonde, and beautiful," Jeanne admitted.

"You *are* beautiful," Lori assured her.

"You like red noses and runny eyes?" Jeanne asked.

"Who does? Think Amanda will let you come back tomorrow?" Lori asked.

"Nope," Jeanne said. "She already told me that there was no sense going back till Monday."

"They're signing up for parts in play-reading tomorrow."

"I wasn't going to try out for Eliza, anyway," Jeanne said.

"You'd be a good Eliza."

"You'll be better." Jeanne knew that her friend wanted the part very much. But since they were both interested in being actresses and were also best friends, it was sometimes better not to compete. They were taking a special English course in play-reading this semester, and since Jeanne had had the best part in the last play they read, it was really Lori's turn.

"I don't know why Mr. Murphy wants to read *Pygmalion* anyway. There's really only one female part."

"He's probably thinking about doing it for the class play."

"But they always do Shakespeare."

Jeanne mimicked Mr. Murphy's extremely cultured voice as she said, "Tradition dictates it."

"If Amanda doesn't let you go to school tomorrow, will you be locked in all weekend?"

"I suppose so. You know how Amanda is." Then quickly, so she wouldn't seem to be complaining about her stepmother, she added, "Conscientious."

"I wish my folks would get a divorce," Lori said. "Only I'd sure want to live with my mother. I've been trying to talk her into leaving. She says there's no way he'd let us, but I wish we could just disappear. Maybe we will."

"You've only got two and a half years and then you'll be on your own," Jeanne said. She always wished there was something else she could say to console Lori about her home life, but she didn't understand why Lori's parents stayed together, either.

"Look how happy your folks are," Lori said. "There's your mother doing her career thing and you've got Amanda to take care of you. You even like your stepbrothers."

"I know. I can remember when I was just beginning to read and all those gruesome fairy tales had witches and evil stepmothers. I would try and figure out how I got the perfect stepmother."

"You're lucky," Lori said.

Jeanne turned to Lori and said, almost angrily, "I know I'm lucky. But you know something? I think everyone has things in their life that they're missing. I'm not satisfied. I *do* want to be thin and blonde and beautiful. It's not a joke. And there's something else — it's like I don't really belong here."

"A stranger in a strange land," Lori said philosophically.

"Something like that," Jeanne said. She drew her knees up under her chin. "Sometimes I look at my hands, or my face in the mirror, or my feet or something, and I think they belong to a stranger. It's like there's really another Jeanne Lee who's quite different from the one you know. It's like. . . ." Her voice faltered for a moment and she added in a softer, more intense voice, "Sometimes I have the feeling that no one really knows me, and what's more, I don't even know myself."

"*I* know you," Lori said certainly. "You're my best friend. You're also one of the most popular girls in the school. And you're talented and you're beautiful even if you don't look exactly like the girl on the cover of that book."

"I could go on a diet," Jeanne said. She reached up and touched her blunt, dark reddish-brown hair. "And I could bleach my hair out to white blonde. I could get blue contacts for my green eyes. I could introduce the world to the real Jeanne Lee."

Lori was laughing now as she said, "Will the real Jeanne Lee please stand up?"

"She's not here," Jeanne said. "The one you see in front of you is an imposter."

Chapter 2

By Sunday morning, Jeanne felt so much better that she decided she could meet her mother for brunch as usual. For the last ten years, ever since her parents' divorce, Jeanne and her mother had a standing date at Balboa Park. When Jeanne was younger they'd spent hours at the San Diego Zoo, but now they usually had brunch in the fancy restaurant and spent the afternoon walking around the park.

This Sunday they had tickets to a play at the Old Globe Theater. As Jeanne was leaving to meet her mother, Amanda said, "Have a good time and say hello to your mother."

"I will," Jeanne promised, and her first words to her mother were, "Amanda says hello." One of the ironies of their family situation was that she always carried a greeting from her stepmother to her mother, but neither of them mentioned her father unless there was a reason to do so.

Mary Lee smiled and nodded, then linked her arm through her daughter's and said, "I'm glad Amanda is such a nice person. It makes what I have to tell you easier."

"You're getting married and moving to Alaska," Jeanne teased, but she felt a sharp pinprick of fear. When she'd been younger, she'd tried very hard to persuade her mother to look for a suitable husband. But she'd long **ago** come to understand that Mary Lee's major interest was her job as a top salesperson for a large machinery manufacturer.

"I *am* moving," Mary said. "That is, I'm moving if you approve."

"Where?" The word stuck in Jeanne's throat. Though she'd long ago adjusted to seeing her mother only once or twice a week, she couldn't imagine not seeing her at all. Her mother was more fun than anyone she knew. Her mother was . . . her mother.

"To San Francisco," Mary Lee said. "I can have a substantial raise *and* my own sales territory."

"And hundreds of thousands of dollars?" Jeanne asked, not at all surprised. It was an old joke between them that her mother's ambition would eventually lead to great sums of money.

"Hundreds of millions," her mother said with a straight face. Then she smiled and shook her head. "It might even mean less money for a while because that sales territory is very competitive. But I would be my own boss and the first woman at Holcomb and Jones to have a whole sales territory to herself. They're talking about making me a vice-president."

"Congratulations." Again, the words stuck in her throat.

"It isn't decided," her mother said. "Let's have our breakfast and we'll talk about it."

"What's to talk about?" Jeanne asked. "I'm fifteen years old and you're certainly not abandoning me on a snowy doorstep or anything."

"Nope." Her mother squeezed her arm. "I'm offering you a free ride to San Francisco whenever you want. Every weekend if you care to commute."

"Every weekend?" Jeanne laughed. "Won't that many plane tickets eat up your raise?"

"I don't care."

"I know. And I'll be proud of you when you take over the whole territory. I can see you now with your six-shooters drawn, saying, 'Boys, from now on this here San Francisco is Holcomb and Jones land exclusively.' "

"You sound just like Clint Eastwood," her mother said.

"I was trying for John Wayne."

They mounted stone steps and walked into the Cafe Del Morro where Mabel, the hostess, greeted her by name. When she'd been younger, the older woman had always patted Jeanne on the head, but now Jeanne towered over Mabel by at least six inches. Each Sunday, the little woman shook her head and said, "Jeanne, you've grown into such a big, strong girl. I just can't get over it. I can remember when you were just such a skinny little thing."

As always, Jeanne smiled at Mabel and pretended that it didn't bother her a bit to have her size discussed with amazement. But inwardly she winced. This Sunday, after Mabel led them to their table, Jeanne said to her mother, "I always feel like she's going to offer me a job as a bricklayer or something. I guess I'm lucky she doesn't ask to feel my muscles."

"She doesn't mean any harm."

"She just means I'm fat," Jeanne said. "I know I'm fat but I wish she wouldn't say so every week. It's apt to spoil my appetite."

"You're not fat." Her mother ignored Jeanne's attempt to joke. "And you are a nice, strong, healthy girl. Be glad of it."

"I'm supposed to be glad that I'm five

feet nine inches tall and weigh a hundred and sixty-five pounds? Mom, why didn't I inherit your body as well as your brains?"

"You're built like your father's side of the family. And you're not fat. You're just large-boned. Come on, let's eat."

Jeanne followed her mother to the buffet table and picked up a plate. She walked down the long table and carefully selected her favorite breakfast foods: chicken livers on rice, scrambled eggs and crisp bacon, and pickled herring. Then she took a sweet roll and a bagel and went back to the table.

Her mother followed with a plate loaded with some of everything: chicken in tomato sauce, enchilada pie, roast beef, plus two sweet rolls, and a neat mound of potatoes with gravy.

Jeanne looked at her mother's plate and then at her own, and shook her head in dismay. "How can I get fat on a third of the calories that you eat in a day?"

"I don't eat this way all the time," her mother answered. "You're getting three delicious meals a day at home. I'm living on yogurt and cheeseburgers." She crunched into a buttered bagel and added, "Besides, your father's family has a slower metabolism rate than mine, and you probably inherited that."

"Dad's not fat."

"He's not skinny," Mary said. "You know who you look like? You look like your great-aunt Mildred. She died in a plane crash the year you were born, but I met her twice. She was a wonder."

"The anthropologist?" Jeanne remembered the photographs of a middle-aged woman with a funny haircut, baggy slacks, and sturdy oxfords. "I don't think that's very flattering," she objected.

"Your great-aunt Mildred was a happy woman," Mary said. "She wasn't afraid to be herself. She had a style of her own. I remember thinking when I met her that I'd never met anyone who was so involved in her work. She could talk about the Philippines for hours and make it sound like heaven. Anyway, she lived for five years in the Philippines and I think she ate mostly boiled fish, but she wasn't thin."

"So where's all that positive thinking you're always talking about?" Jeanne grumbled. "Aren't you the one who's always saying that I can be anything I want? Now you're telling me I'm going to end up looking just like Great-Aunt Mildred. Thanks a lot."

Her mother placed her hand over Jeanne's and said quietly, "I don't have to take this job, Jeanne. When I first started with Holcomb and Jones, I was the only woman salesperson and I thought I had to grab every chance. But I can wait till you're ready for college."

"Are you going to give up your big chance just because I'm feeling a little sorry for myself?" Jeanne asked. "It's not your fault I look like Great-Aunt Mildred, you know. I mean, you were young and in love when you met my father. I'm sure you checked for the usual heredity problems," Jeanne tried to joke. "Who expected you to ask about thick ankles or slow metabolism? Not me. So go to San Francisco and send me a ticket in a month. I'm going on a diet and the next time you see me, I'll look just like Rosalinda Revere."

"Rosalinda Revere?" Her mother didn't know who Jeanne meant, but she seemed relieved that Jeanne had fallen back into her usual flip way of handling problems.

"She's the heroine of the worst of three romances I read last week. Come to think of it, that's probably why I seem a little peculiar today. I read so many of those romances that my mind's turned to vanilla pudding." Jeanne stopped to stifle a laugh. "Oops, I said the unmagic words. No more vanilla pudding for me. From now on, it's boiled fish."

The rest of the day went too quickly,

especially watching the comedian Frank Sutton as Falstaff in the play at the Old Globe. Of all the regular actors at the Old Globe, he was Jeanne's favorite because he always managed to make his dramatic roles just a little funny and his comic roles just a little sad.

"I'm going to miss you," Jeanne said to her mother suddenly, with a catch in her voice. "You're the only adult I know who takes my acting seriously. Even Mr. Murphy doesn't think I have a real chance at an acting career."

"You can do whatever you want, Jeanne. You've got talent."

It was a standard Mary Lee answer and usually it was reassuring, but this morning Jeanne was full of doubts. "Mr. Murphy treats my ambition like a sickness I'll get over. And he's supposed to know good acting."

"Mr. Murphy probably didn't want to be a teacher, you know. He probably wanted to be an actor. So he may be disappointed by life and taking it out on you."

Jeanne ruffled her hair and tossed her head and said in a theatrical voice, "*I've* been disappointed by life."

"Never," her mother said and hugged her. "You've got everything it takes to make a success of life, kiddo."

Jeanne tried to hold onto that thought when they parted at seven-thirty that evening. As she kissed her mother on the cheek, she asked in a casual voice, "When are you leaving?"

"I'm flying up to San Francisco on Wednesday," Mary said. "That is, if you're sure you can get along without me."

"I'll love having some place to visit during Easter vacation."

"You can come a lot more often than that, I hope."

"Sure, but Lori and I are thinking about taking a Saturday modeling class at the YWCA. We figured it would be some sort of preparation for our acting careers. It's supposed to teach stage presence, and there are voice lessons."

"I'm glad you have Lori," her mother said. "And Amanda."

"And Dad and Hank and Tim," Jeanne reminded her. She was surprised that her voice caught on the last sentence. She hugged her mother quickly and left.

At home that evening, Jeanne announced, "Mom's moving to San Francisco. She got a promotion."

Her father and stepmother looked at each other, and her father cleared his voice and said, "You'll miss her."

"Yes," Jeanne agreed, staring at the floor.

"Dear . . ." Amanda began.

Somehow, just from the tone of her voice, Jeanne knew that more bad news was coming. She felt something twist in her stomach as she waited.

"Lori called long distance right after you left today. She said to tell you that her mother and she left town last night. She said her mother was divorcing her father, and they were in Colorado. She'll write you as soon as they're settled, but she didn't leave an address or phone number. And they don't want her father to know she called."

"She always said they should get a divorce," Jeanne said. There was a lump in her throat and she couldn't think of anything else to say. She stood up and walked toward the kitchen, asking, "What did you guys have to eat?"

"There's some chicken in the refrigerator," Amanda answered. "Didn't you have supper?"

"Not much," Jeanne lied. She'd had a cheeseburger and a slice of cake with ice cream, but all of a sudden she was ravenously hungry again. She would have to begin her diet tomorrow, since this day was ruined.

Chapter 3

School was definitely different without Lori, but the worst of the pain went away after a couple of weeks. Jeanne kept busy, stayed active, and tried not to notice the dull pain that ran through her days like a toothache.

She got the part of Eliza in *Pygmalion*, but since there was no real competition, she didn't feel any special pleasure from it. However, doing something that she could put her whole self into felt good and she soon discovered that she was able to play the tough-sweet English woman without letting her personal mood enter into it.

The best part of her days was the hours when she sat in the dark theater reading Eliza Doolittle's lines over and over. She learned to use hard work as an anesthetic in those first days, but without Lori and her own mother nearby, there was always the sense of emptiness around her like a gray haze.

Jeanne's class performed the play-reading in a special assembly for the freshmen and sophomores on a Friday afternoon. Jeanne knew she was better than she'd ever been, reading the part of Eliza with a broad cockney accent and making her voice something between a song and a screech.

Since it was just a reading and there were no costumes, no sets, and no movement on stage, the performers were all surprised at how responsive the audience was. At the end they clapped a long time, and Jeanne had to take three bows all by herself. As Jeanne stood on the stage, bowing, she felt truly happy. She grinned out at the audience, enjoying every moment of the applause. Then she recognized her stepbrother and his two best friends, waving at her proudly. She waved back and yelled out across the auditorium in Eliza's screeching voice, "Eawwh ... there's me brither!"

People turned and laughed as they waved back, happy to be recognized.

Jeanne kept the wonderful feelings all the way through Friday night and Saturday. She enjoyed hearing Hank tell the family how great she'd been. And when Amanda insisted she read some of the play for them, she rose from the dinner table and got her script. They all laughed at her rendition of Eliza, and Amanda said, "You have a real talent, Jeanne."

Jeanne looked at her father, hoping he would also praise her. Her father said, "You sounded great, Jeanne Bug."

Tears welled up in Jeanne's eyes at the sound of that old nickname. He hadn't called her Jeanne Bug since she'd been a very small child. It reminded her of the days when he and her mother had still been married, and thinking about that faraway happiness made her throat ache.

"I'll have another piece of pie," she said. "I deserve a second slice after all the work I've done."

Amanda said nothing as she put the last piece of pie on Jeanne's plate, but the look on her face told Jeanne exactly what she was thinking. Her stepmother was biting her tongue to keep from mentioning the weight that Jeanne was gaining.

The next morning at breakfast, Amanda said, "I'm joining Weight Watchers today and I want you to come with me."

"You're not fat," Jeanne answered. It was the only thing she could think of to say.

"I've put on about ten pounds in the last five years," Amanda said. "If I keep that up, I'll be fat at fifty."

"People are *supposed* to be fat at fifty," Jeanne said.

"Fat is unhealthy," Amanda answered quickly. "The meeting is at four o'clock at the Presbyterian Church. We can walk."

"I don't want to go to Weight Watchers."

"Come with me this one time," Amanda pleaded. "It will be fun. And you know I'm shy."

Jeanne shook her head and said, "Now don't go using child psychology on me, Amanda. I know you're not shy and I know you don't need to go to Weight Watchers."

"I do — and Jeanne, you're much too young and pretty to let being overweight spoil your future."

Jeanne laughed and said, "Maybe you should write ads or do commercials or something. I can see you on TV right now: 'Girls, is ugly fat spoiling your brilliant future? Polish it off with these little meetings. Confess your sins, abandon your evil ways. . . .'"

Amanda was quiet until Jeanne stopped her mock commercial. Then she asked, "You don't want to go with me this afternoon?"

"No, I don't."

"Then I'll go alone."

"Why don't you?"

It was as close as they'd come to fighting in the years they'd lived together. Jeanne managed to say, "Listen for me," in a light voice as her stepmother left the room, but the mood of the day was ruined.

Jeanne went to the movies all alone that afternoon with five dollars worth of popcorn, Cokes, and candy. Amanda didn't mention the meeting that night at dinner, but when she served baked chicken, green beans, and salad for supper, it was easy for Jeanne to eat lightly since she'd stuffed herself at the movies.

Later that evening, she wrote a long letter to Lori, telling her all about the play-reading and everything else that had been happening at school. She put it in a shoebox with the other letters she'd written her best friend. If Lori ever called or sent a letter with her return address, she'd wrap them all up in one package and send them to her. Even if she never heard from Lori again, it felt good to write.

Chapter 4

Amanda mentioned Weight Watchers several times in the next few days. Jeanne ignored her until Sunday morning when Amanda cornered her and suggested she come to the meeting that afternoon.

Jeanne flushed, but she kept her voice steady as she said, "I know you think that's going to solve all my problems. But I just can't imagine getting up there in front of people and talking about how I got fat because I stole too many cookies from the cookie jar but I'll never do it again. . . ."

"It's not like that. You should just come to one meeting and see what it's really like," Amanda said eagerly. "The woman who leads it is cute and funny. It's all jokes and everyone is nice to each other. She talks more about liking yourself than anything else."

"I like myself just as I am," Jeanne said,

and opened the refrigerator door to find something to eat for breakfast.

"I think you must have put on at least five pounds since your mother left . . . " Amanda began.

"Ten," Jeanne corrected her. She closed the refrigerator and walked toward the kitchen door. Before she left, she said in an extremely dignified voice, "Please don't disturb me. I have to read all of Shakespeare's sonnets this morning."

Once in her room, she dug out the box of red licorice sticks she had hidden in the bottom of her closet and opened the historical novel she was halfway through. She was really annoyed at the way Amanda kept nagging her.

Her mother called about an hour later and asked her to skip school on Friday and fly up to San Francisco late Thursday afternoon for the weekend. After they'd arranged the details, her mother asked, "Are you all right?"

"Never been better."

"You sound down in the dumps."

"Never down in the dumps," Jeanne responded. "Always fat and sassy." "Fat and sassy" was what her great-grandmother had called her when she was a baby, and now they used it as a family expression for everything being just right. Only in her case, Jeanne mused, it was a little too close to the truth now.

Packing for the San Francisco trip put Jeanne in a bad mood because she couldn't fit into her best dress, and the sweater and skirt she finally decided to take for dressing up looked tight. She made a face at herself in the mirror and said, "You starve next week!"

Her mother was so glad to see her when she arrived that she was actually crying. Jeanne hugged her and said, "Hey, you're a big girl now, remember?"

"I was thinking you might decide to go to college at Berkeley," her mother said. "You could live with me and commute."

"It's nice to be wanted," Jeanne said. "But I'm not planning to go to Berkeley. U.C.L.A.'s the place for a brilliant, budding actress like me. You know I've got to be close to Hollywood in case I get discovered."

Jeanne put her hand on her forehead and threw back her shoulders in imitation of a glamorous actress. "Dahling, I was just sitting there on that little ole stool in that little ole drugstore and this nice man in a Rolls Royce came up to me and offered me the leading role in his new giant movie."

Her mother hugged her again, laughing and crying all at once. "You are the funniest, most wonderful girl in the world. I don't know what I did to deserve such a beautiful daughter."

"Please, let's not pry into your deepest, darkest past," Jeanne replied, hugging her back.

"Okay. Here and now, how about Chinese food for dinner? We'll have the most expensive things on the menu. This is a real celebration. And the food is delicious."

The celebratory dinner was the first meal Jeanne had really enjoyed in a long time. It was great to be away from her stepmother's watchful eyes and worried expression, and she had three helpings of everything. Finally, she sighed and said, "This is my idea of heaven."

"Sweet and sour ribs and almond duck?" her mother teased. "Don't they feed you down there in San Diego?"

A faint shadow passed over the perfect evening, but Jeanne laughed and shrugged. "You can see by looking that I haven't been exactly starving, but this is the best Chinese food I've ever eaten. Do you live close to here?"

"Wait till you see my apartment," her mother said. "It's on the third floor, it's tiny, and it costs a fortune. You'll have to sleep on the couch."

"That's all right," Jeanne said, and she meant it.

Her mother's apartment *was* tiny. The main room was large enough to hold a couch and big comfortable chair in front of the TV. Besides that, there was a table and four chairs nestled in a bay window alcove. "This room was the nursery in the original mansion," her mother said. "My bedroom was the maid's room, and all I can say is that they must have had very small maids in those days. I could only get a single bed in there."

"Where's the kitchen?" Jeanne asked.

"Open those doors," her mother pointed to two wide folding doors that Jeanne had assumed closed off a closet.

She opened the doors and laughed aloud. There was a small sink, a smaller stove, and three cabinets. The counter was so small that her mother's blender and microwave just about covered it all. "I'll bet you eat out a lot," Jeanne said.

"That or frozen dinners in the microwave. The oven doesn't work."

"It's kind of cute."

"I'm glad you like it," her mother said dryly. "Wait till you see the bathroom."

"Another closet?"

"Another closet."

"So where do you hang your clothes?" Jeanne asked.

"There was a large storage space originally used for children's toys," her mother answered. "It's now the most compact and efficient closet you could ever hope for."

"I think it's a cute apartment," Jeanne said. "And you're right downtown."

"That's the point. But I hate to think of you having to sleep on that couch. I was going to buy one of those pullout sleepers, but there isn't any room to pull it out. And they're never very comfortable, anyway."

"Don't worry about me," Jeanne said. "I'll get by."

But sleeping on her mother's couch turned out to be quite a complex problem. Jeanne wrestled with every possible arrangement; she tried putting her feet over the arms, then curling into a ball, then sleeping with her knees bent. It seemed as though every position she tried was slightly more uncomfortable than the last one. About midnight, she gave up and moved to the floor.

Her mother woke her early in the morning by gently poking her with her foot. "Get up and go into my bedroom. You can get a couple of hours of comfortable sleep while I do some work."

Jeanne rolled over, then stood up. "What time is it?" Every bone in her body ached from sleeping on the hard floor.

"It's six-thirty. I'll wake you at nine and we can go to the park."

"I'm too old for the park," Jeanne grumbled.

"No one is *ever* too old for Golden Gate Park," her mother promised. "Now get into my bed and sleep for a while."

Her mother's small, single bed felt truly luxurious. Jeanne stretched and turned and fell into a deep, full sleep immediately. It was almost eleven before she woke and went into the living room where her mother was working at the table.

"You should have wakened me," Jeanne said.

"I tried twice but you were determined to sleep." Her mother laughed. "You had some hard things to say about my floor. We'll get you an air mattress today."

"Where will you store an air mattress? You don't have room for another thing in this apartment."

"I'll deflate it when you leave and put it under my bed. Go ahead and shower, and I'll take you to brunch."

The shower stall was so narrow it was almost impossible to turn. When Jeanne was dressed and ready to go, she said to her mother, "Your apartment is so small that I feel like one of those giants in *Gulliver's Travels*."

Her mother's face fell and she said, "I want you to be comfortable here. I want you to visit often."

"I will, Mom, I promise." She hugged her mother again and said, "Now let's go out and see the world."

They rode the cable car down to the edge of the water and found a wonderful restaurant that was built out of several cable cars linked together. From their table they could see all of San Francisco Bay. Jeanne ordered pancakes, bacon, and eggs, and said, "I worked up a real appetite wrestling with that couch last night."

"Appetites are mostly habit, Jeanne." Her mother cut into the melon she'd ordered.

"That's easy for you to say," Jeanne answered. "You never did eat much. Dry toast and melon for brunch. Ugh."

"I already had yogurt and instant oatmeal at home," her mother laughed. "You should see your face — don't you like oatmeal anymore? You used to love it when you were a little girl."

"Could we talk about something else? I'm trying to enjoy my pancakes."

"Of course," her mother said. "I want to

have fun this weekend. I'll take you to Golden Gate Park for tea. Then tonight we'll go to the theater and tomorrow I thought we might drive down the coast to Carmel. It's the prettiest spot in the world. And we have to pick up that air mattress and I'd like to buy you some new clothes today. Get you some really smart city rags. There's a wonderful shop right down the street from here. Very chic."

"Sounds great," Jeanne said happily.

"It will be," her mother promised, as she signed for the check. "Now let's go shopping. I see you in purples and blues."

Jeanne was still happy when they went into the shop, but her mood changed very quickly as her mother pulled one outfit after another off the rack and asked her to try them on. "I know they won't work," Jeanne said. "They look small and they'll make me look fat."

"Just try one," her mother urged. "They're all so stylish."

"I'll try some of the shirts and pants, but I refuse to even put on those knit things."

"All the girls are wearing them."

"Not all the fat girls," Jeanne said.

"You're not fat," her mother insisted.

"Then why does everyone look at me and roll their eyes heavenward?" Jeanne imitated a snooty look on a salesgirl's face, and her mother laughed and pushed her into the dressing room.

An hour later they were both ready to admit defeat. Few of the things that she and her mother picked were big enough, and those that did fit made her look monstrous. Finally, she said, "Mom, let's face it. I'm just not built for these things. I'll stick to my plain old skirts and sweaters."

"Let's try the department stores," her mother said. "All these things are made in Hong Kong and their idea of a large isn't very large at all."

"I hate to shop for clothes," Jeanne said. "I thought we were going to have fun."

Her mother looked at her quietly, with an expression very much like the one Jeanne had become accustomed to seeing on Amanda's face. But her mother only said, "Okay. You'd be beautiful in rags. You're my girl."

"A face and figure only a mother could love . . ." Jeanne began to joke, but the words stuck in her throat and she turned her head away.

"Let's get the air mattress and go to the park," her mother said quickly.

A few minutes of the natural beauty of Golden Gate Park restored Jeanne's usual good humor. She put the disappointment of the shopping trip behind her and let herself slip into a sort of hazy silence as she walked over little stone bridges, through fallen leaves and paths lined with small rocks.

There were so many flowering bushes and plants that Jeanne had to remind herself that this was all real. At one point she said, "I keep thinking Disneyland has added something to the Magic Kingdom and that if I reach out and touch the blossoms, they'll be crepe paper."

"It's real," her mother answered, and they walked in silence for a long while.

Jeanne loved the park. She felt more contented than she had in weeks, partly because walking in the park reminded her of earlier times when she and her mother had spent every Sunday at Balboa Park in San Diego. At four-thirty they stopped for tea in the Japanese Tea Garden of Golden Gate Park.

As she sipped her tea and looked around her at the flowering pink trees and the elegant Japanese pagoda, Jeanne sighed and said, "It's almost as beautiful as Balboa Park, isn't it?"

"We've had some great times there, haven't we?" Tears came to her mother's eyes as she asked, "Jeanne, is it too hard for you having me up here?"

"I miss you, but it's not *too* hard. I only saw you on weekends anyway."

"I miss you more than I could have thought possible," her mother said quietly. "But I knew you would be growing up and leaving me soon, anyway. And I thought it was important to take this promotion when it was offered."

"Mom, we went over all this. I'm one hundred percent behind you."

"But you look so unhappy," her mother said.

"Unhappy? Me? I'm happy as a lark," she said, trying to sound breezy.

Her mother shook her head and said, "Jeanne, a mother can see things that no one else can. And we can both see you've put on weight. I've been doing a lot of thinking and I've decided I'm going to ask for my old job back."

Jeanne put her hand over her mother's and said, "Mom, I don't want you to move back to San Diego. I miss you, but after high school I'm leaving for the stage, the bright lights. It would make me feel guilty to leave you behind if I know you dumped your career for me."

"You're just being sensible. Instead of feeling guilty, why don't you try to feel loved?" Her mother laughed, but the words were serious.

"I *do* feel loved," Jeanne said, slumping in her chair.

"People who feel loved don't overeat," answered her mother.

"Why can't you just let me work out my own problems?" Jeanne tried very hard to keep her voice level and not let the hurt show. It seemed that everyone kept coming back with the same criticism about her weight. Why couldn't people just accept her as she was? "You've never nagged me before. Why start now?"

"I'm not nagging. I'm just telling you what I know."

"What do you know?"

"That you miss me a lot more than either of us guessed."

"So you think if you move back to San Diego I'll suddenly get thin and beautiful? Don't you think I've managed pretty well without you all these years? I haven't lived with you since I was five years old, so I must have made some adjustment. I managed the divorce. Why don't you think I can manage this?"

Jeanne saw her mother's face was draining of color, and knew that her words were harsh. She softened her voice. "Of course I miss you. I love you. But I'm a big girl now."

"You're only fifteen. You've had enough

trouble in your life without being totally abandoned by me. If only your father. . . ." Her voice trailed off and she didn't finish her sentence.

"What about my father?" Her mother never said anything about her father at all.

"If only he were more emotionally supportive," her mother said. "I know you get a lot from Amanda, but I wish your father were more help."

"Daddy is supportive in his own way," Jeanne said. "You just never understood those long silences."

"You're right," her mother agreed promptly, but without a lot of conviction. "He's a fine man and he's made Amanda happy."

"And I'm happy, too, Mom. I do miss you, and it didn't help to have Lori move the same week you did. I was sort of in shock for a while, but I'm getting on top of it now. So don't worry. You just think I'm unhappy because I put on a few pounds. Next time you see me I'll look so skinny you may not even be able to see me at all. I'm going to Weight Watchers with Amanda."

"Really? Why didn't you tell me?"

"Because I just decided. She's been after me for weeks to go on a diet with her. So far, her nagging has just made me hungrier, but I'm going to my first meeting on Sunday. I promise."

"You don't have to go on a diet for me. It's for yourself," her mother said.

"I agree. So can we just drop the dramatic scenes and have fun for the rest of the weekend?"

"Yes." Her mother sighed.

"And can I have all the ice cream I can eat until Sunday night? With none of those 'Oh my dear, I'm so concerned' looks from you?"

"Ice cream *and* cake," her mother promised.

"With fudge sauce," Jeanne added. "Live, eat fudge sauce, and be merry, for Sunday I diet."

Chapter 5

Weight Watchers wasn't anything like what Jeanne expected. In the first place, the women at the session were all so happy and cheerful and seemed so old that Jeanne really felt out of place. Even though several of them made a point of saying something encouraging to her as they waited to be weighed in, they all sounded patronizing, as though it were cute for a teenager to have a weight problem. Jeanne supposed they meant to be friendly, but it didn't make her feel better.

The best thing about the meeting was that the woman who weighed her didn't say anything at all. She simply gave Jeanne a little card with the date and her weight written on it. Jeanne looked at the number, saw that it said 179, and quickly put it in her pocket.

She tried to tell herself that the scale

was rigged to make people weigh more than they really did. But finally, she admitted that the scale was probably right. She'd been weighing herself in the morning in her cotton bathrobe, and her scale had been hovering around 174. The difference was probably clothing and the time of day.

There was no doubt that she needed to lose weight. There was also no doubt that most of the people who were at the meeting believed that Weight Watchers was helping them lose. Amanda introduced her to a woman named Doris who had lost 60 pounds. It was hard for Jeanne to imagine how Doris must have looked before she went on the diet, because she was so short.

It seemed to take an awfully long time to weigh everyone in. Jeanne wondered why there wasn't a more efficient system; she also wondered why the leader of the meeting, whose name was Anna Marie, had on so much makeup and such a fancy dress. She looked very out-of-place in San Diego on a Sunday afternoon.

Jeanne did try to listen, though. Amanda was right that the meeting seemed to be as much about accepting and loving yourself as it was about choosing foods. Anna Marie talked in a voice that was a lot like the voices the cheerleaders at school used at pep rallies.

Anna Marie punctuated her lecture with questions and comments from the audience. She opened the meeting with, "Any success stories today?" When anyone volunteered a comment, Anna Marie would beam at them and say, "Good, good," and everyone would clap.

Jeanne didn't clap because she didn't like being forced to act cheerful. She might have to diet but she certainly didn't have to pretend she liked it. Though Anna Marie kept talking about how delicious all the recipes in the new cookbook were, Jeanne knew they weren't going to taste a thing like the ice cream and cake and fudge sauce she'd had for dinner the night before.

Because she was new, she had to stay after the meeting and have the eating program explained to her. She had the Weight Watchers booklet, and Anna Marie went over the way to measure food and how to make choices. "After you finish the first few weeks, you'll have a whole series of choices, but right now we keep it simple."

Jeanne looked down at the lists of allowed food, and smiled. It was simple, all right. For the next week, she was going to be living on carefully measured amounts from seven short lists. Never mind, she was determined to do it.

"The goal weight we've given you is

temporary," Anna Marie said. "Eventually, you'll establish your own goal, but this gives you something to look at and consider."

Jeanne looked at her card and saw that 145 was written beside the temporary goal. She shook her head. If she was going to have to live on lettuce leaves for the rest of her life, she was going to get a lot thinner than 145. She wanted to be 130 pounds and she was determined to do it. What was another 15 pounds after she'd lost 34? Besides, it would be a lot more exciting to lose 49 pounds. In fact, she decided she would aim for 129 so she could say she'd lost 50 pounds.

The idea made her smile and Anna Marie said, "You may think that goal is too high or too low. Don't make a judgment yet. Give yourself time to get used to the program and find out what your body really needs and wants."

"My body wants chocolate-fudge sundaes," Jeanne joked.

"Listen carefully and you'll discover your body wants to be healthy," Anna Marie answered. "It's your *emotions* that urge you to eat sugar. When you get an urge to overeat, say to yourself, 'Life is sweet.'"

Jeanne got a very clear picture of herself

wheeling up and down the candy aisle of the supermarket, muttering, "Life is sweet," and she burst out laughing at the idea.

Anna Marie smiled patiently and said, "Just follow the program this week, and don't expect to learn it all in one meeting."

Jeanne did follow the diet program all week. It wasn't as difficult as she'd imagined because she was excited about the prospect of losing a lot of weight. She was hungry a lot of the time, but she fed herself with daydreams about the day when she would be a beautiful, slim star of the theater.

School was hardest because most of the kids either didn't eat at all or ate thousands of calories. The first day in the cafeteria line, she took the large bowl of salad that the diet called for, but it tasted kind of dull and mushy because it wasn't refrigerated, and she wasn't sure the dressing was on the lists. The next day she just packed a half sandwich and a piece of fruit. That was easier, even though Anna Marie had expressly warned that she should eat large quantities of vegetables. Better to starve than turn into a bunny rabbit, Jeanne thought.

Amanda was very good about preparing menus that included her special dishes. But mostly, Jeanne felt like the food she was eating wasn't really food at all. It was almost as though it didn't count, it was so unsatisfying next to a hot fudge sundae.

On the next Sunday afternoon, she was quite nervous as she stepped up on the scale to be weighed. The woman who took her card and wrote down her weight smiled briefly and said, "Good for you."

Jeanne found a chair beside Amanda and sneaked a quick look at the weight record. It said 176. That meant she'd lost three pounds!

Amanda whispered, "How much did you lose?"

"Three pounds."

"That's wonderful!"

Jeanne turned to stare at her in amazement. "What's wonderful about three pounds?" she asked impatiently. "I starved all week to do it and I could go out and have two ice-cream sundaes and put on five."

"You've got to learn to recognize success," Amanda said. "I've only lost five pounds in four weeks. You managed three your first week. What did you expect?"

Jeanne didn't answer because she wasn't sure *what* she had expected. It was silly to think she could starve one week and get to her goal weight, but in her heart she was disappointed that it was going to take so long.

Anna Marie opened the meeting with the same old question, "Any successes?"

Several women reported losses smaller than Jeanne's, but she didn't raise her hand. Amanda whispered, "Aren't you going to tell?"

Jeanne shook her head. Three pounds wasn't success. When she was truly slim, *that* would be success. Nothing else was going to make her feel good about herself. She was going to keep focused on the long-term goal, and when she got there she would feel wonderful.

Chapter 6

Two days later, Jeanne ate two cheese-burgers at lunch, and on the way home from school she stopped and had ice cream with two other girls who were in her drama class. Though she felt terrible about breaking her diet, she rationalized that it was time she made some new friends who were interested in dramatics.

They weren't as much fun as Lori, but Kathy and Darla were both nice girls and they laughed at Jeanne's jokes almost non-stop. As Jeanne ate the last spoonful of her ice-cream sundae, she said, "I know I'll regret this tomorrow, but it sure was fun while it lasted."

"It *was* fun," Kathy Murdock agreed. "We could walk home together again tomorrow afternoon."

Jeanne frowned. "Not unless you promise to detour around the mall by at least five blocks. I have no willpower."

"We always stop here," Kathy said.

"Life's not fair," Jeanne said. "*I* never stop here, and look at how thin *you* are." She thought Kathy must be about a size seven. She was small and cute and very nice. Some girls did seem to have it all.

Kathy and Darla were nice enough, but they didn't have anything to say in response to her jokes. When she left them Jeanne realized they hadn't really said much at all. While an appreciative audience was gratifying, it wasn't like a real friendship with someone like Lori, who could hold her own in any conversation. For the thousandth time, she wondered if Lori would ever write. The shoebox full of letters to her friend was almost full and Jeanne still hadn't heard a word.

On Wednesday she went back on the Weight Watchers program, and she managed to stay on it until Thursday evening when Kathy called and invited her to come to dinner. Jeanne agreed and when she got to Kathy's house she discovered that dinner was pizza and salad. She told herself it would be rude not to eat a little pizza. Three slices later, she felt stuffed and guilty.

When she got home, Amanda called out, "Have fun?"

"Sort of," Jeanne mumbled.

"What did they have to eat?"

"Pizza and salad," Jeanne answered. When she saw Amanda's worried look she snapped, "You don't need to look like that. I just had salad."

"Then why do you have pizza sauce on your T-shirt?" Hank asked in a laughing voice.

Instead of laughing, Jeanne stormed out of the living room and slammed the door as she entered her bedroom. About an hour later, her father knocked at the door and she let him in.

He cleared his throat and sat down on her dressing table stool. Then he cleared his throat again. He seemed so nervous and uncomfortable that Jeanne almost wanted to laugh. The idea of having a long heart-to-heart talk with her father after all these years was out of the question. She knew how hard it was for him to talk about personal things. Finally, she decided she would have to help him out. "You came in here to tell me to be nice to Amanda and Hank. Right?"

"Not exactly," he said. "I just wanted to remind you that we're all a family."

"Okay. We're all a family," Jeanne agreed. "So I don't have to be nice to Hank and Amanda?"

"Yes, you do," he said, and frowned. "I don't know how to talk to you anymore, Jeanne. You're so . . . so flippant."

"Tell Amanda not to nag me," she said. She wanted to add that he'd never known how to talk to *anyone*, but she was afraid he'd never try again if she said that. He meant well, she supposed, so she also supposed he should be encouraged.

"Amanda has been a good mother," he said.

"Amanda has been a good *step*mother," Jeanne agreed without hesitation. "But Amanda worries a lot about how she looks and now she's worrying even more about how *I* look. Daddy, I don't want to spend the rest of my life staring in the mirror."

He seemed to consider that. His face, which was as square as hers, seemed to grow longer as he puzzled over what to say next. She watched as he wrinkled his brow, pursed his lips, winked his eyes, and opened and shut his mouth. If he hadn't been her father, his expressions might have made her laugh. As it was, she wanted to cry. Why couldn't he loosen up and talk to her?

Finally, after a very long silence, he stood up, kissed her on the forehead, and said, "You're a good girl. I know you'll do your best to get along."

Jeanne didn't reply. As he left the room,

she went to the dressing table seat and looked in the mirror. She wrinkled her brow, pursed her lips, winked her eyes, and tried to imitate every one of her father's attempts to communicate. A good actress might someday need to have such a set of expressions in her repertoire.

She was still making faces at herself when Hank called her to the telephone. As she started to the door, he added, "It's Lori. She's in Michigan."

Jeanne ran to the telephone. "Lori? Is that really you? Where are you?"

Lori's tone was distant. "Michigan. Jeanne, has my father called you?"

"Twice, but I didn't know where you were. He still doesn't know where you are?"

"I've had such a hard time convincing Mom that it would be all right to trust you. I'll give you my address, but don't give it to anyone at all. Not even your stepmother or brothers. All right?"

"All right. I guess it was bad, huh?"

"I'll write and tell you someday. He's always been mean, but that last week was awful. So we ran and it's taken this long for either of us to feel safe."

Jeanne shuddered. How lucky she was to have the sort of home she had. She might laugh at her father for being noncommunicative, but he didn't have a mean bone in his body. And she'd never doubted for a minute that he loved her.

She wrote down the address that Lori gave her, and asked, "How is it? Are you in school?"

"Of course. And I've got the lead in the class play. We're doing *West Side Story* and I play Maria. And guess what? I'm in love. His name is Michael Dougherty and he's an actor. Isn't that something?"

"Is he in love, too?"

"Yes. And we've decided to go to New York City together when we graduate. It's so romantic. . . . I miss you, Jeanne. Mike is like you . . . sort of a joker, too. Only he's got a serious side. He's sensitive and handsome, too. I wish you could meet him."

"Handsomer than David Green?" Jeanne teased. She was happy for her friend but it hurt just a little bit to hear how well she was doing. While Jeanne had been moping around missing Lori, Lori had been making new friends, getting a boyfriend, and winning the lead in the class play.

"David," Lori laughed. "I'd forgotten all about him."

"So I shouldn't give him your address, even if he gets down on his knees and begs me for it?"

She laughed louder then, and said, "I'd like to see David get down on his knees and beg you for *anything*. You'd make a funny-looking couple."

"I don't know why you say that," Jeanne said. She couldn't really think of a joke to go with that statement.

"I've got to go," Lori said.

"Will you write back when I write?" Jeanne asked.

"When I have time," Lori promised. "Send me a letter."

"How about a shoebox full?" Jeanne asked.

"You're funny, Jeanne. I miss you." Lori hung up without saying good-bye.

Jeanne held onto the receiver for a while, missing her friend. Then she hung up, went to the hall closet, took out her jacket, and said, "I'm going for a walk."

"Now?" Amanda asked. "It's dark outside."

"I'll walk Tray," Jeanne said. "Then I'll be safe."

"I already walked him," Hank said.

"Come on, Tray," Jeanne said. But the dog just looked at her and wagged his tail. It made her sad to see how old he was getting. Everything made her sad tonight.

"I'd rather you didn't go out alone," Amanda said. "Hank, you can walk with her."

"Nope," Hank said. "I'm in favor of

women's liberation. Jeanne will be safe. She's a big, strong girl."

"Hank . . . " Amanda began, but Jeanne was already out the door.

She walked fast, letting the cool night air hit her face and calm the heated flush of emotion that she wore. She wasn't certain why finally hearing from Lori had been so disappointing, but it had. And Hank really got on her nerves these days. She wished it was like the old times, when she and Hank and Tim had been really good buddies. But Tim was in college now and only got home once in a while, and Hank seemed to enjoy making her feel awful just for the fun of it.

As she walked, she cooled off a bit. She was sorry that Kathy Murdock was too dull to be a really good friend, but those were the breaks. Mostly, she just missed her mother and Lori more than she had expected. But it was time to grow up and be independent. What was it her mother always said? "You can choose how you feel. You always have a choice."

While Jeanne walked, she tried to think of pleasant things, and not to think of anything that hurt. She even said out loud, "You can be anything' you want to be, Jeanne." Then she answered herself, "Anything but thin and beautiful."

Abruptly, she switched her course and

started toward the mall, where she bought six candy bars. She ate three of them very slowly on the way home and then went directly to her bedroom. She put the other three at the bottom of her sweater drawer. Emergency rations, Jeanne told herself, and went to bed without brushing her teeth or washing her face.

The next morning when she weighed herself (even though Anna Marie had said they should only weigh themselves once a week at the meetings), she saw that she'd put on two of the three pounds she'd lost. She shrugged, brushed her teeth, and smiled at herself in the mirror. At least she was seeing direct results. If you didn't eat, you lost weight. If you cheated, you gained. Well, she would stay on the diet from now on and she'd lose.

Her fourth period diet lunch was harder to eat than ever, and by sixth period when she went to drama class, she was absolutely starving. She was glad they were between productions and Mr. Murphy would dismiss them on time. When they were rehearsing, they stayed until four or five o'clock.

She tried to concentrate on the lesson, which turned out to be nothing more than reading Shakespearean sonnets aloud.

Though he'd threatened to make everyone memorize at least twenty poems this year, the truth was that Mr. Murphy was a very easy classroom teacher. It was only when he was directing a production that he insisted on hard work. The classroom part of the drama course was a snap.

Today it was David Green's turn to read his sonnets. David was usually very quiet and he didn't take a very active part in the class as a rule. Jeanne had never really seen what it was about him that attracted Lori, but he could read well, and though he put very little expression into the words, his deep, mature voice gave the sonnets a resonance that Jeanne enjoyed.

"Eye contact," Mr. Murphy commanded.

David raised his eyes and looked straight at Jeanne. She smiled at him, hoping a friendly face would encourage him to plod along in spite of Mr. Murphy's interruptions. " 'For thy sweet love remember'd such wealth brings / That then I scorn to change my state with kings.' " His voice trailed off as he finished the poem.

He smiled at her and she smiled back. She forgot her complaining stomach in her enjoyment of the way the sun slanted in the window, making David's hair and skin look golden. And his eyes were very blue, so blue that she was surprised she'd never noticed them before.

"That's better," Mr. Murphy said. "Now do this one with good eye contact and I'll let you go."

David looked straight at her as he half read, half recited his last poem. As she watched him, letting the words flow over her and enjoying the beauty of the sunlight, she felt herself get dizzy and it occurred to her that she might be sick.

Poor David! If she should suddenly have to run from the room, Mr. Murphy would probably make him recite ten more sonnets. She did her best to keep her eyes steady and not disturb his recitation.

He was on the last part now, which she'd heard many times before because it was one of Mr. Murphy's favorites. But it sounded very different as David said the words: " 'Then come and kiss me, Sweet and twenty, / Youth's a stuff will not endure.' "

He sat down and Jeanne thought she might really faint from hunger. Her head was light, her heart was beating fast, and she felt as though something funny was happening in her chest. She was sure she was sick.

The worst part was that she followed

David with her eyes as he sat down. She hoped he didn't notice, because he would think she was foolish. Just because every girl in school had had a crush on David at one time or another, he'd probably think that was what was wrong with her.

She tried to turn her head away but she couldn't help it. He was the best-looking boy she had ever seen. After being in the same classes with David Green for ten years, she finally figured out what Lori thought was so special about him.

She realized she wasn't getting sick. She had just fallen in love.

Chapter 7

It was exciting, scary, and silly, but it didn't go away. When she woke in the morning, the first thing she thought about was David. When she dressed for school, she tried to pick her prettiest clothes. She stared into the mirror for a long time, trying to imagine that David could love her in return.

At school she seemed to always know exactly where he would be, and with just a few minor alterations in her routine, she was able to say hello to him at least five times each day. And in drama class, he usually gave her a smile and sometimes a few words about the lesson.

But it was pretty clear to Jeanne that David wasn't a bit more interested in her than he had been in Lori. Her heart sank every time she thought about how many years Lori had suffered from unrequited love. Now she knew how it felt, and she wished she could replay all those years and offer her friend support instead of laughter.

Perhaps because she was afraid someone would laugh at her, she didn't tell anyone how she felt about David. Once or twice she brought up his name when she stopped for ice cream with Darla and Kathy, but it was clear that they didn't have any particular interest in him.

One day David came into the ice-cream shop and ordered a chocolate cone. Darla called out, "Hi, David."

He turned slowly and smiled at them, but he didn't call any of them by name. When he left, Darla said, "I think he's cute."

"Do you have a crush on him?" Jeanne asked.

Darla shook her head and said, "No, but Kathy does."

"I do not," Kathy said quickly.

"Lori did," Jeanne volunteered. "But he never paid any attention to her at all." She felt kind of guilty for betraying a confidence about Lori, but it really hadn't been much of a secret.

"A lot of girls are that way about David Green," Kathy explained, and her voice said clearly that she was bored with the subject.

But the subject of David didn't bore

Jeanne one bit. When she saw David, she saw a very special, almost magically attractive person. It was as if that golden light she'd seen when he was reading in front of the classroom followed him wherever he went, even though no one else seemed to see it.

Everything David did took on a new significance. The day he said, "Pretty sweater," Jeanne walked on air for at least two hours.

She began to understand words in a new way, too, and she woke on the morning of her sixth day of being in love obsessed with the word *enchantment*. The word had a meaning she'd never truly appreciated before, and she even wrote something about it in one of her letters to Lori:

"I think being in love is truly enchanting because you see the whole world in a very special way."

Being in love with David had definitely helped her stay on her diet. When she went to Weight Watchers that week, she had lost five pounds and was down to 173. Anna Marie complimented her in front of the whole group, even though Jeanne hadn't raised her hand to report on her success.

After the meeting, Amanda said, "Next week is my last week for a month. I've been at goal weight for six weeks, so I just weigh in once a month to make sure I stay there."

"You were at goal weight when you came in," Jeanne said, but she was teasing, not complaining.

"Besides, your father and I think you'll do better on your own. I tried to stop nagging you this week and you did very well."

Jeanne smiled, barely paying any attention to what Amanda was saying. She was busy calculating how much weight she had to lose before she'd be brave enough to really let David know how she felt about him.

During the next few days, Jeanne studied David out of the corner of her eye. Yes, he was probably just about the same height and weight as Tim, who'd told her he weighed 148 pounds. That meant she had more than 20 pounds to lose before she weighed less than David. She sighed and turned her thoughts to the class lessons. It would take a lot of hungry days to get down to 148, but she knew she could do it.

During the next month she did lose another 13 pounds and she began to like the way she looked in the mirror. Her cheekbones showed a little bit and she experimented with darker and lighter shades of makeup to make the hollows even more pronounced. The happiest day came when she visited her mother in San Francisco and said, "I'd like to go clothes shopping if you still want to buy me some things."

They picked out a dressy, golden silk blouse and a bright blue silk skirt that was almost ankle-length. She also selected several cotton shirts and skirts. On the way out of the store, she stopped by a rack of knit pants and touched a bright, mustard-colored pair longingly. "Want to try them on?" her mother asked.

"Not yet," Jeanne said. "Ask me in another thirty pounds."

"You're not planning on losing that much more, I hope?"

"Yes, I am." Jeanne said.

"I think you're thin enough right now." Her mother frowned. "How much do you weigh?"

"I weigh nine pounds less than I did when you left town. So I have a way to go, don't I?" Jeanne said.

"I think you're about right. You have big bones." Her mother frowned again.

"I'm not even at Anna Marie's temporary goal weight," Jeanne answered. "Trust me."

"I'll trust you for another five or ten

pounds," her mother said. "Then we'll talk about it."

Jeanne shook her head. "I just can't please you, can I? Last time I was here, you nagged me because I was too fat. Now I'm too thin. Only I'm *not* too thin, Mother. Look at these clothes. Size fourteen. Is that the size of a girl who's starving to death?"

"The whole conversation is a setup to see if I can talk you into going back to Wing Wing for more Chinese food," her mother finally joked.

"Great!" Jeanne said, "Chinese food isn't even very fattening."

But when they got to the restaurant Jeanne watched what she ate. She talked her mother into ordering one combination dinner with a side order of steamed vegetables because she didn't want to gain back one ounce of the weight she'd lost.

Three weeks later the woman at Weight Watchers who weighed her said, "You're getting close to your goal weight."

"That's not my *real* goal," Jeanne said. "I want to lose another twenty pounds at least.

"You'll have to talk to Anna Marie about that," the woman said.

"I don't have to have Anna Marie's permission to lose weight," Jeanne snapped.

The woman didn't say anything else. She just handed Jeanne her card and Jeanne sat down. As usual, Anna Marie started the meeting by asking, "Any success stories today?"

Jeanne was getting so she enjoyed watching the progress of some of the older women, but she still felt like an outsider because she was so much younger than all of them. There was one young mother who looked like she might be eighteen or nineteen, but the baby that she held during the meetings kept her from talking to anyone at all.

After the meeting, Jeanne walked home by way of the mall, daydreaming about the time when she would finally get David to really notice her. Because she had read and seen so many plays, her daydreams were often just like stage plays that ran through her mind. She imagined herself in a hundred different situations and costumes. She saw herself on the Kansas plains as a pioneer girl. Then she saw herself as an Egyptian princess all covered with gold and jewels. She could see herself very clearly in gingham or with golden snakes on her wrists, but her imagination failed her with words. The dialogue never changed much.

David always said something like, "I

never noticed how beautiful you were before. Where have you been all my life?"

"I've been right here waiting for you, my darling."

In her dreams, when David took her in his arms to kiss her, she was always very slim and much shorter than he was. In real life, she knew that they were about the same height and weight. But one day soon, she would be much thinner and then her height wouldn't be so noticeable.

She walked by the ice-cream parlor where she used to stop with Darla and Kathy until she persuaded them to switch to the pizza parlor where they could get ice cream and she could have a Diet Coke. The smell of the cold sweets tempted her, but just for a minute. She was feeling much too good about how she looked to jeopardize it with junk food. And while she knew that ice cream would eventually be a part of her maintenance plan, she wasn't anywhere near her goal weight. Let others eat sweets. She would rather be beautiful.

But she couldn't resist a glance inside the place, and what she saw shocked her so much she stopped dead-still and looked again. David was in there — with Kathy Murdock. They were sharing an ice-cream cone. One would take a bite and then laugh and hand it to the other. They looked like they were having a wonderful time. David Green — and Kathy Murdock!

Jeanne walked away as fast as she could, hoping they hadn't seen her staring at them. Why hadn't Kathy told her about David? Was he dating Kathy or had they just bumped into each other and decided to share an ice-cream cone?

What hurt her the most was how happy David had looked. It made her want to cry out, "David, why didn't you wait for me?"

Then the truth crushed her as she realized that she would never be as little and cute as Kathy, no matter how long she dieted. She would always be a "big, strong girl." David, obviously, preferred a very different type.

When she entered her house, Amanda asked, "How did you do?"

"I thought you weren't going to nag me," Jeanne snapped and went to her room. Then she shut and locked the door and went to her sweater drawer. Rifling around under the papers that lined the drawer, she found the three candy bars that she'd hidden a while ago. Then she sat down on the side of the bed and began eating the chocolate bars, slowly and methodically, with tears running down her cheeks.

Chapter 8

Kathy called her on Wednesday evening to tell her that David was her new boyfriend. Jeanne gripped the telephone so tightly that her knuckles were white as she listened to Kathy rattle on about what a great guy David was. Kathy didn't really want her to talk much, she just needed a listener. That was good, because Jeanne couldn't think of anything nice to say.

"David is just so sweet," Kathy said. "He called me out of the blue, and I'd never really noticed how handsome he was before. Did you ever notice how blue his eyes are?"

"Not really," Jeanne lied. She could close her own eyes and reproduce the color of David's anytime she wanted to. But there was no point in letting Kathy know that. No point at all.

She didn't see much of Kathy or David that week because she deliberately changed her route in school so she wouldn't have to watch them walking hand-in-hand to classes. But there was no way to avoid seeing the way they looked at each other in drama class. They sat on opposite sides of the room, but Kathy spent all her time looking at David.

Jeanne watched Kathy watching David. Kathy looked absolutely darling with her tiny little heart-shaped face cupped in one little hand. Kathy always wore thin gold chains around her neck and now she was wearing a slim gold bracelet that made her wrist look smaller and more delicate than before.

Jeanne decided with just a little effort, she could learn to hate Kathy Murdock. Then she reminded herself that that was absolutely ridiculous. Kathy was a nice girl and David was a nice boy, and they hadn't done a thing to her. So why should she hate them?

When she weighed in on Sunday night she was back up to 152 pounds and she knew it was because she had tried to drown her disappointment in overeating. She promised herself she would stick to her diet even if it killed her the next week, and she did pretty well until Friday night when she went to the movies with Darla.

Darla ate two candy bars and a big box of buttered popcorn and Jeanne had a Diet Coke and a box of plain popcorn during the movie. But when the movie started getting boring, Jeanne went out to the candy stand and bought a big box of red licorice sticks, which she put in her purse for later.

As she tucked them away in her purse it occurred to her that she was turning into a secret eater, like a lot of overweight people. She'd always thought it was silly to hide and eat because people could tell by looking at you that you ate too much. But since she'd started dieting, she almost never ate fattening things in front of other people.

That Sunday evening, she weighed in at 155 and she really felt discouraged. The woman at the scales, whose name she'd discovered was Pearl, said, "Maybe you ought to stay after the meeting and talk to Anna Marie."

"What good will that do?" Jeanne asked.

"She might be able to help you," Pearl answered.

Anna Marie gave her a food chart to keep during the week. "All you have to do is write down everything you eat, and that will make you more aware of what you're doing."

Jeanne took the food chart but she had no intention of filling it out. The last thing she wanted to do was let Anna Marie see a list of the cookies, candy, and hamburgers she was eating on the sly.

Even though she didn't use the food chart, just having it around took all the fun out of her binges. On Tuesday, two days after the meeting, she unwrapped a candy bar and took a big bite. Then she threw the rest in the trash and promised herself she wouldn't eat anything at all until she lost some weight.

That evening at dinner she ate only a few bites, even though she was really hungry. She was determined to make up for the empty calories she'd been eating the last few days.

"You're not eating anything," Amanda said.

"I'm not hungry."

"That broiled chicken and green beans are good for you. It's foolish to eat junk food and skip meals, Jeanne. Foolish and dangerous," Amanda warned.

"How do you know I eat junk food?" Jeanne asked. She was furious with her stepmother for bringing up dieting at all.

"You're not eating much at home and you're gaining weight," Amanda said. "It doesn't take a genius to know you're eating somewhere else."

Jeanne felt her temper rising. "Amanda,

why don't you mind your own business?"

"You *are* my business," Amanda said. "I love you, Jeanne, and I want you to be happy."

"I *am* happy," Jeanne insisted.

"Then why this compulsion about food?"

"Leave me alone. You're not my mother!" Jeanne ran from the dining room to her bedroom, certain she'd hurt Amanda's feelings.

No one knocked on her door that evening and nothing was said the next day about the argument. She ate almost nothing the next few days and no one mentioned a word about that.

The way Amanda tiptoed around her to avoid confrontations drove Jeanne crazy, and she got crankier and crankier with her stepmother. It didn't help that she was so hungry all the time that she felt like she had a starving tiger growling in her stomach. She lost weight fast that week because she ate so little. But things were so strained with Amanda that on Thursday Jeanne called her mother about going to San Francisco for a visit. Her mother was concerned, but eager to have Jeanne come the next weekend.

Her father drove her to the airport. When he dropped her off, she had the distinct impression that he was glad to see her go. He kissed her good-bye and said, "Have fun."

"I will," Jeanne promised, and she was determined to do exactly that. Two weeks seemed plenty long to suffer over a boy who didn't even like you, and she was determined to find some way out of the bad mood she'd been in.

"How's everything?" her mother asked as they walked out of the airport toward the car.

"Couldn't be better," Jeanne replied.

"Not what I heard," her mother said quickly. "I might as well tell you that Amanda called when your father took you to the airport. She's really upset about the way you two are getting along."

"*Aren't* getting along," Jeanne corrected. "You know Amanda. She tries too hard."

But Mary Lee was unsympathetic. "I don't really know Amanda and maybe you don't, either. That poor woman said that maybe it was all *her* fault that you were so unhappy. Jeanne, what are you doing to her?"

"It's not my fault she nags me all the time," Jeanne said defensively.

"Is it true you've stopped eating?"

"No, it's not true," Jeanne snapped.

"Can't you tell by looking at me that I'm eating just fine?"

"How much do you weigh?" her mother asked.

Jeanne was getting short. "None of your business."

"Oh, yes it is, young lady. How much do you weigh?"

"This morning? Stripped? I weighed one fifty-five. Does that seem like the body weight of someone who's suffering from malnutrition to you?"

"No. How much did you weigh before you started dieting? The first time you visited me here?" Jeanne's mother pressed her.

"I weighed one seventy-nine on the Weight Watchers scale at night, but in the morning at home I weighed one seventy-four."

"So you've actually lost nineteen pounds?"

"Yes, actually, I have."

"Good for you, Jeanne, I'm proud of you."

The praise released a storm of tears. Jeanne felt foolish, but it also felt good to cry. They got into the car and her mother waited silently while Jeanne blew her nose and then sobbed out the words, "Amanda watches every bite I take. And one minute she's on me about eating too much, and the next minute she claims I don't eat enough. I can never please her."

"That's what she says about *you*. That she can never please *you*," Mary Lee said soothingly.

They looked at each other and then began to laugh. Mary Lee handed her a Kleenex and said, "Maybe you should both try and let up on each other. Amanda's obviously trying too hard to be the perfect stepmother. And you're pushing yourself pretty hard if you've lost nineteen pounds in a little over two months."

"Of course I've gained and lost some of the same pounds," Jeanne said.

"That's what's bothering Amanda the most — the seesaw effect, she called it."

"The trouble with being a teenager is that you don't have any privacy," Jeanne said. "If I were twenty-three and living on my own, no one would know if I was losing straight away or on a seesaw."

"But the point is that you *are* a teenager, and you need good nutrition."

"You sound just like Amanda," Jeanne said.

"We have a lot in common," Mary Lee said thoughtfully.

Jeanne laughed at that idea. Her mother seemed so strong and independent, and

Amanda seemed just the opposite. Then she said, "You both married Daddy, so I guess you have *something* in common. And you both have to put up with me."

"Jeanne, I don't put up with you. I want you to know that I find being your mother a real joy. You're a very special person. Amanda thinks so, too. That's one of the things she said, that she hoped you would learn to see yourself as you truly are."

"I'm afraid that's what I'm doing," Jeanne said. "And I guess that's not a lot of fun."

"What do you see?" her mother asked.

"A big, strong girl," Jeanne joked. And then she broke into tears again.

This time, her mother hugged her and patted her head as though she were a very small girl. Then she started the car and said, "When you really learn to see yourself, you'll see beauty, brains, and talent, all rolled up into one glorious package, my dear."

Jeanne drew away and blew her nose again. Then she said, "Oh, yeah? What if you're the only one who can see that? What if I really do have a face that only a mother could love?"

"Is that what this is all about? Boys?"

"Maybe," Jeanne admitted. "I've never had a boyfriend. Maybe I never will."

"You can believe anything you want. You can *be* anything you want."

"I can't be a Kathy Murdock."

"No, of course not. But what does she have that you don't?"

"Kathy is little and cute," Jeanne said.

Her mother drove in silence for a long while before she said, "If you spend your life looking at what you can't have, you'll never really discover what you can have. What happened to that acting career?"

"I'm still working on that. But I think Mr. Murphy is going to have us do *Romeo and Juliet*," Jeanne said.

"So?"

"So can you honestly see me as Juliet?"

"Why not?"

"Because I'm not little and I'm not slim. I'm not the romantic-heroine type."

"Maybe you should give yourself a chance to try out for parts before you turn yourself down," her mother said dryly.

Even Jeanne had to laugh at that wise advice. Then her mother turned into her neighborhood and said, "I'm finding this conversation a little circular at this point. And I'll tell you the truth: I just spent an hour on the telephone with Amanda, so I'm ready for some fun. How about you?"

Jeanne laughed and asked, "Isn't that called closing the sale?"

"What do you mean?"

"Isn't that what they teach you to do at Holcomb and Jones? Work the client over and then close the sale. I can almost hear you handing me the pen and saying, 'Sign on the dotted line,'" joked Jeanne.

"What do you think I'm signing you up for?" Her mother was smiling, but her voice sounded suspicious.

"The short-order course in happy living or something like that. Or a book called, *How To Get Through Your Teenage Crisis Blindfolded.*"

Her mother steered the car onto her street. "You're doing fine with your eyes open, Jeanne. Just fine."

"I feel fine," Jeanne said. She finally relaxed, ready to have a great weekend and confident that she was going to be able to handle whatever came next.

Chapter 9

Jeanne memorized most of Juliet's lines on
the flight home from San Francisco. And
that evening, she called Darla and asked
her if she'd start playing tennis with her
after school every afternoon. "I want to
lose some more weight," Jeanne said, "and
I think exercise will help."

"Sure. I didn't know you could play
tennis," Darla said.

"My brother Tim taught me two years
ago. I was never very good, but I'm going
to get better."

"I'm good," Darla said. "Maybe I can
give you some pointers."

Jeanne knew it wouldn't be easy to concentrate on tennis when she was hungry,
but she was determined to stick to her diet
and exercise even if she *did* feel like she was
starving all the time. And she had to admit
that she was pleased with how much better

she looked in shorts than she ever had before.

That first afternoon, Darla said, "You've lost weight, haven't you?"

"Yes," Jeanne told her.

"How much?"

"Not enough," Jeanne answered. "One of these days I'm going to be slim."

"You look okay now," Darla said.

"Actresses have to be thin or they don't photograph well," Jeanne answered. "And I'm a long way from thin."

"You're not the type," Darla said. "I mean, you're built kind of . . . square."

"You really know how to hurt a girl," Jeanne said lightly. But Darla *had* hurt her and she had to turn away quickly to keep it from showing. Funny how emotional you could be when you were starving all the time. One minute she was so proud because she could get into size fourteen shorts, and the next minute she despaired of ever wearing a smaller size.

"I mean, you're just sort of. . . . You have square shoulders and you're tall," Darla said slowly, trying to soften her words.

"I think you're trying to say I'm big," Jeanne said dryly. "Or did you mean fat?"

"Not fat." Darla shook her head quickly. "I was trying to give you a compliment but now I wish I'd just kept my big mouth shut."

"Not to worry," Jeanne said. "One of these days I'll be standing sideways and you won't be able to see me. Or you'll think I'm a fence rail or something."

"You've always got a joke," Darla said. "That's why people like you so much."

"That's me," Jeanne agreed. "Jeanne the Jokester. Come watch the fat lady in the circus laugh, kiddies."

"Don't say that," Darla protested. "I never called you fat."

"You didn't have to," Jeanne agreed. "Facts are facts and the facts are — " She stopped herself, suddenly remembering something Anna Marie had said in one of her lectures. According to Anna Marie, a lot of overweight people had a problem accepting compliments because they needed to believe bad things about themselves so they would have an excuse to keep on eating.

At the time she'd heard that, Jeanne had thought it was nonsense. But wasn't that sort of what she was doing right now? Instead of going on with the jokes, she changed her voice and said, "Thanks, Darla. I'm glad you think I look better. I've been trying hard."

"You look really normal," Darla said.

"I have no intention of being *normal*,"

Jeanne said in a dramatic voice. "I intend to be simply devastating . . . to have men dropping at my feet, to have rubies and pearls and gold strung around my neck, to have the Taj Mahal for my summer cottage. For plans like that, you can't look normal. You must look stunning."

They were still laughing when they started their tennis game, and Jeanne actually enjoyed playing. When their time was up, she noticed a group of three boys standing over at the edge of the court, and was pleased to see that they were looking at her. She walked just a little bit taller and straighter than she would have before as she went to the clubhouse. Having boys notice her was fun.

On Wednesday, Mr. Murphy announced that tryouts for *Romeo and Juliet* would be in a week and a half. Jeanne groaned inwardly as she calculated how much weight she would have to lose in order to look slim enough to play Juliet. It was getting hard to lose even a pound a week and she was still a long, long way from the weight she had hoped for.

She remembered the way the boys at the tennis court had looked at her the day before, and that gave her courage to raise her hand when Mr. Murphy asked who would be trying out for Juliet. He raised one eyebrow quizzically when he called out her name, but he wrote it down without making any comments.

Only three boys had raised their hands for Romeo, but every girl in drama class except Kathy raised her hand for Juliet.

Mr. Murphy raised one eyebrow and asked, "Miss Murdock, you don't care to compete for the fair crown?"

"No," she answered.

"Why not, may I ask?"

"I'd be too nervous," Kathy said. "Besides, it's a lot of lines to memorize."

"Yes, it is." Mr. Murphy frowned at the class and said, "I suggest all of you more ambitious damsels start memorizing the part now."

Mr. Murphy made everyone who was going to try out for Romeo agree to try out for at least one other part, but he said to the girls, "You can try out for the nurse, if you want. Otherwise, I'll assign the small parts and the rest of you can be in the battle scenes."

The girls groaned. One brave girl actually complained aloud. "Why did you pick a play with so few female parts?"

"Because we always do Shakespeare for the class play, and in Shakespeare's time women didn't go on the stage. A boy like

David, with his face, would probably play Juliet instead of Romeo."

Some of the rowdy boys in the class laughed very loudly. Jeanne looked at David's face and knew he was dreadfully embarrassed by Mr. Murphy's words. How could a teacher be so insensitive?

She walked out of class with David and Kathy, and one of the boys who'd laughed earlier said to David, "So long, Juliet."

David flushed and grabbed the boy by the elbow and asked, "What did you say?"

Kathy looked frightened and backed off, but Jeanne reached out and put her hand on David's arm. She said, "Let it go, David. He's not worth the trouble."

David did let go of the boy, who immediately scurried away without looking backward. Jeanne laughed and said, "You should see your face. You look exactly like Clint Eastwood. That poor kid won't say anything like that again."

"It's not *him* I'm mad at," David admitted. "I wish I'd punched Murphy in the nose."

"He'd deserve it," Jeanne agreed, "but then you'd be the one suspended, not him."

"I don't think I'm going to try out for Romeo after all," David said.

"Give it a few days," Jeanne counseled, "then decide."

David paused and looked at her with a new expression. Then he said, "Thanks, Jeanne. I might have been suspended for fighting by now if it wasn't for you."

"You're welcome," Jeanne managed. This was real praise, and she had the feeling that David was seeing her as an individual, not just Kathy's friend, for the first time. It felt good, like the sun was shining brighter than usual.

"Want an ice-cream cone?" David asked. "I'll treat."

Kathy tugged at his arm and said, "You said we could go to pick up my new dress."

"I have a tennis date," Jeanne said quickly. "But thanks anyway." She was feeling better about herself than she'd ever felt. Nevertheless, she was still not exactly thin at 150 pounds and she would certainly rather play tennis than watch Kathy try on a size-seven dress.

David nodded. "See you tomorrow. At the drama class trip to Old Globe — remember?"

"I'd almost forgotten," Jeanne said. "All that excitement shook my head loose."

"I wish I could go," Kathy said, "but Bernardi won't postpone her test. She said chemistry was important and drama was a frill."

"Why don't you come later?" Jeanne asked. "Even if you miss the backstage tour, you can hear the lecture." One part of her was hoping that Kathy wouldn't come on the field trip because it would mean she would have a chance to be alone with David. Another part of her knew that wasn't fair. The nicest part won the internal argument, but not without a struggle.

"I really don't care that much," Kathy said. "You guys can tell me about it anyway."

"Save me a seat on the bus," David said to Jeanne.

"Yes," Jeanne said and went to her tennis date with Darla with the sweet promise of spending tomorrow afternoon with David all alone.

Chapter 10

Even though she had attended many Old Globe Theater productions, Jeanne found the backstage tour fascinating because she'd never been behind the scenes. Some of the equipment was simply an advanced version of the San Diego High School stage, but much of it was so sophisticated that even their guide didn't completely understand it.

More than once, Jeanne asked what some mechanical contraption was used for, and the guide shrugged. She was better on the history, though, and had obviously memorized the major events of the fifty years that the theater had been in Balboa Park.

The guide, a very young woman who identified herself as an actress, seemed to spend most of her time leading tours and running errands. Jeanne asked how she had gotten her job at the Old Globe.

"I started as an apprentice when I was a freshman in college. And I just hung around, making a pest of myself until they actually hired me. Not that they pay me much. I'd be better off at Burger King," she replied.

"But you're learning things," Jeanne said.

The guide sighed and said, "Yes and no. I do a lot of boring stuff and it's pretty clear I'm no actress, so I think I'm going to get a real job pretty soon."

"Then your job will be open?" Jeanne asked eagerly.

David, who was standing right beside her, laughed and said, "You going to drop out of high school and be an actress, Jeanne?"

"They won't hire you," the guide said. "But you should try out for the apprentice program. You might get on for the summer."

"I thought they only took college students," Jeanne said.

"Once in a while they take a mature-looking high school student. Check it out."

Before Jeanne had a chance to bristle at the suggestion that she was a mature-looking high school student, the young woman turned to the group and said in her tour-guide voice, "So now you've been behind the scenes, and the next time you see Peter Pan flying through the air, you'll know where the wires are coming from. Is the magic gone forever?"

Several students smiled and said yes. Jeanne said no. For her, the magic of theater included the *whole* theater — backstage, the costumes, and the actors themselves. To be part of that magic was the thing she wanted most in the world.

The guide pointed to the door and said, "Go out there and then enter the auditorium from the regular door. There's someone waiting for you on the stage who'll bring the magic back."

In the auditorium Jeanne immediately recognized her favorite actor, Frank Sutton, even though he was fully costumed. He greeted them from the stage as they entered, and she was thrilled that she was going to get a chance to talk to him.

Jeanne felt as though she was seeing an old friend, partly because he was wearing the Falstaff costume from *The Merry Wives of Windsor*, the play that she'd seen with her mother just before she moved. He had a huge false nose, a wiry beard, and hair that stuck out in all directions. His cheeks were painted bright red and his belly was stuffed so that he looked a little like Santa Claus in March.

He started out by asking in a deep, rough voice, "Any of you know who I am?"

After a minute of silence, Jeanne said, "You're Frank Sutton."

He laughed and rephrased the question, "Anyone know what character I'm playing?"

She gave the others a chance to answer, then said, "You're Falstaff from *The Merry Wives of Windsor.*"

"Right you are. And who are you?"

"Jeanne Lee."

"Well, Jeanne, why don't you tell your classmates what *The Merry Wives of Windsor* is all about."

Jeanne laughed and shook her head. "I saw it twice but I'm not sure I know what it was about. I'm certain I couldn't repeat the plot."

"Do you often see the same play twice?" the actor asked.

"I try to."

"And you liked *The Merry Wives of Windsor?*"

"I like everything I've ever seen you in."

"Indeed? You've got excellent taste for a young person. I suppose you plan to go on the stage yourself someday."

Several people in the class laughed and Jeanne suddenly remembered that she wasn't alone with him. She said in a quieter voice, "Maybe."

"Maybe? Come along! You'll never make it into the spotlight with good manners. If you want to get ahead in the theater, you'll have to learn to leap up on the stage and pursue the smell of greasepaint."

Several people were laughing now. Jeanne felt her face flushing, and she hoped that David wasn't one of them. She said no more and Frank Sutton began to recite his prepared talk about the Old Globe, telling them a lot about its fifty-year history. Jeanne listened avidly as he also reeled off a list of actors who had performed on the stage.

He talked a lot about physical presence and how posture could make so much difference in how an actor looked. He showed them how to hold their hands upward to look younger and downward to look older. Walking across the stage several times, he demonstrated different walks for different characters.

At one point he talked about how important size was on the stage and he said, "Most actresses are smaller than most screen stars or models. That's partly because only the tall ones look well in photographs, but it's also because so many parts call for carrying the dead heroine off the stage. We have a joke that is a series of questions. Who is the most perfect actress to play Desdemona? Ophelia? Juliet? And so on. . . . The answer is always Helen Hayes because she is only four feet eleven and weighs less than one hundred pounds."

Most of the kids in the class laughed at the joke, but Jeanne didn't because it didn't seem the least bit funny to her. How could she ever hope to be a success in the theater if she weighed half again as much as the actress who was perfect for every part she yearned to play? And where would she find leading men tall enough to play opposite her five feet nine inches? It wasn't funny at all.

It took Jeanne a few minutes to regain her self-control and ask, "How important is the play, I mean, how much do the words you have to say have to do with your talent?"

"Very little," he said. Then he looked at his watch and said, "We have about ten minutes left. How would you like it if I gave you an acting lesson?"

"Sure," several students answered. But when he asked for volunteers, only Jeanne clambered onto the stage.

He reached out to help her up and then

said, "I can see you learn fast. No more 'maybe' from you, right?"

"Right." She tried not to let her nervousness show. After all, there was no one out there but the kids in the drama class, and they'd all seen and heard her before. But just the fact that she was actually standing on the Old Globe stage made her knees tremble.

"Let's play a love scene," Frank Sutton said. "I'll need another volunteer."

There was a long silence, then some whispered voices. Jeanne stared down at her feet, mortified. Then David climbed onto the stage and everyone yelled things like, "Look out for Kathy," or "Here comes Romeo."

"The thing about a love scene is that it all depends on the mood," Frank Sutton said. "Most lines that lovers say are very simple. Something like, 'I love you,' usually does the trick. So that makes it very tricky to convey the impression of complex emotions you want to give."

David was smiling at her as though he thought the whole thing was a joke. She tried to concentrate on what the actor was saying, but she couldn't help thinking as much about David as about acting.

Frank Sutton said, "I want you to say,

'I love you,' to each other as many different ways as you can think of. Be happy, sad, glad, mad, wistful, deceitful, whimpering, bragging, threatening, whatever. Each time, change your voice level, your mood, your expression. Let's see what kind of actors you really are."

David and Jeanne stared at each other. Then Jeanne took a deep breath and said, "I love you."

"I love you," David responded.

Several kids laughed, but the actor quieted them by saying, "Anyone who thinks he can do the job better can volunteer. Just line up over there and we'll give you a chance behind the footlights." His dare had the required effect and the audience became deathly quiet.

It seemed strange, but it wasn't unpleasant to stand on that stage and repeat the same words over and over. Eventually, Jeanne found that she had almost hypnotized herself. She reached deep into her chest for a throaty voice, then raised her chin and trilled a young girl's voice. On and on she went, exhibiting a range of moods that impressed even her.

David's responses were less varied, but he, too, seemed to be trying very hard to express every range of emotion he could think of as he repeated, "I love you," over and over.

"Now kiss," Frank Sutton commanded.

She saw David raise his eyebrows just a bit, and understood that he was surprised and not particularly pleased by the command. But he stepped forward and kissed her on the lips as the class once again hooted with laughter.

She turned in a daze to face the other students, and listened as their laughter turned to applause. Then she asked the old actor, "Can we go now?" It was impossible to look at David.

"No. Wait." The actor turned to David. "Thank you, young man. You did a fine job." Then he said to Jeanne, "I think you may be an actress in a schoolgirl's disguise."

"Really?" Some of the color was returning to her face. After all, David had volunteered to play the scene with her, so he couldn't have minded too much. And surely no one would ever know how difficult it had been for her.

"Perhaps," he said. Then he turned to the class and said, "Now you have me, a stubby and sixtyish character in a funny costume. We'll do the same scene and you'll understand how little words have to do with theatrical meanings." He whipped around quickly and shouted, "I love you!"

Jeanne reacted immediately to the cue of his mood. She put her hands on her hips and bent forward, pursing her lips before she shouted back, "I love you!"

They improvised a comic scene with Frank Sutton chasing her around the stage, as though he were going to kiss her, and each of them shouting different variations of "I love you."

Jeanne found she enjoyed hamming up the words immensely. There was a freedom and joy in playing opposite a real actor, and none of the anxiety that she had felt across from David. Of course, it was easier to be funny than romantic, anyway. And she had an instinct for it because just at the right moment, Jeanne stopped running away from the actor. She turned and faced the actor and shouted, "I love you." She shook her fist as though she were Judy in the *Punch and Judy Show*, and shouting, "I love you," again, she started to chase the actor.

By this time the drama class was making so much noise as they laughed and hooted that Mr. Murphy started clapping his hands in the air to restore order. Everyone took it up and clapped and clapped for the performers. Holding hands, Jeanne and Frank Sutton took three bows.

Frank Sutton said, "What you just saw was a demonstration of the kind of perfect timing that comics seem to come by naturally. Some people could go to acting school for ten years and never be a bit better. Let's give Jeanne another round of applause."

Jeanne turned to face the audience, enjoying every moment of the applause. She felt warmed inside by the praise of her classmates, and she glowed with hope. Maybe she really *was* good.

Frank Sutton led her to the edge of the stage, and as she jumped down, he leaned over. Then he said in a very dramatic stage whisper, "You're talented."

"Talented enough to try out as an apprentice this summer?" she asked.

He nodded briefly and said, "Get your parents to call me in May. I'll arrange an audition."

Jeanne felt as though she were flying as she walked toward the school bus. He had said to call in May. It was almost April now. So she had only a month to wait. And during that month she would do everything she could to prepare. She would diet and exercise, she would try out for the school play and get the part of Juliet. She laughed with joy as she planned exactly how she would conquer the world.

Chapter 11

Some of the glow stayed with her. So many kids told her how good she had been on the stage the next day that Kathy complained, "It sounds like you were the only one on that stage. Wasn't David good, too?"

"He was," Jeanne agreed.

"I know the difference between me and real talent," David said. He smiled at her and she felt as though her heart would break with love for him. David was such a thoroughly nice person, and so good-looking. It wasn't hard to understand why Kathy and she both were crazy about him.

She sighed and turned away from them, starting toward the school exit. "Don't you want to come with us?" David asked. "I'm buying."

"I've got a tennis date," Jeanne said.

"You're getting really thin," Kathy said, and she smiled in the way that annoyed Jeanne rather than pleased her. "And Darla says you're getting good at tennis.'

"That's me, Jeanne the Jock," she answered, but she didn't really like the patronizing way Kathy praised her weight loss in front of David. It was as though she were saying something like, "Keep up the good work, kid. You'll never be any competition, no matter what."

Later, on the courts, Jeanne was still annoyed enough to hit the tennis ball harder and stronger than she ever had before. After the first game, Darla laughed and said, "You're turning into a tiger."

"I still hate the game," Jeanne confided. "But it's easier now that I've had a few lessons from you."

"Looks like your friend wants to give you some lessons today. He's really early again." Darla pointed to a tall, sandy-haired young man who usually showed up on the courts about the time they finished one set and were switching sides. Because they'd seen each other every day for a while, they were at the point where they were exchanging a few words when he came onto the courts. During the last few days, he'd been coming earlier each day.

"He's really early today," Jeanne said. "We have another half hour signed up." They had paused at the net and were whispering to each other, careful not to let the young man know they were watching him watching them.

"I wonder which one of us he likes," Darla mused. "I'll bet it's you."

Jeanne laughed and tossed her head. "No doubt he's fascinated by my famous serve. The lobbed loaf, I believe they call it."

Darla ignored her joke. "He watches you the most. Why don't you ask him what his name is?"

"Let's play," Jeanne said quickly. The last thing she was going to do was speak to some stranger she didn't know. Even the thought of it made her nervous.

He stood and watched them all their alloted time, then Darla called out to him, "Our time's up. Your partner's not here yet?"

"Not yet," he said. "You can keep the court for a while."

"I have to go," Darla said. "But Jeanne will hit a few balls with you. What's your name?"

"Richard Smith," he answered promptly. Then he turned to Jeanne and said, "I think I know your brother, Tim."

"You do?" Jeanne was sure she'd never seen him before she'd noticed him watching her on the courts. She would have remembered his sandy hair and the way he held his head slightly to one side and looked so interested in everything. He certainly wasn't handsome, but he had a nice, eager quality that she would not have forgotten.

"Tim and I were on the track team together," Richard said. "I was a year behind him in school. So you're Joanne Wilson, right?"

"Wrong," Jeanne laughed. "Tim's last name is Wilson. Mine is Lee. And I'm Jeanne, not Joanne. But I'm surprised you were that close." Darla waved good-bye and disappeared as Jeanne said, "You must have a good memory."

"Tim talked about his family more than most guys do," Richard said. "And I remember thinking he was lucky to have a sister and a brother that he liked."

"You hate yours?" Jeanne asked quickly, and then wished she could have resisted a wisecrack just once.

"Only child," Richard answered. "Just me and my dog."

"I'm an only child, too," Jeanne said. "Or I used to be. Of course, my dad remarried when I was little and I got Hank and Tim. But before that, I mean."

"That's two things we have in common," Richard said.

"Two?"

"Being only children and bad tennis players," Richard said.

"Are you really bad?" Jeanne asked.

"Really bad," he assured her.

"Then let's play," she challenged with a laugh.

Richard was better than she was, but not really very good. His aim was off, though he could drive the ball with a fierceness that made Jeanne's arm ache when she returned his shots. It was more fun playing with him than with Darla, because his wild shots gave them both something to laugh at.

After the first set she asked, "Isn't your friend coming?"

"Which one?"

"Any one," Jeanne answered. "The guy with the curly hair. That red-haired girl?"

"You've been watching me," Richard said. He was smiling and Jeanne decided she liked the way his grin was sort of tilted, as though smiling threw the features of his face into a slightly different relationship.

"I watch everyone," Jeanne answered.

"That's three things in common."

"What?"

"Curiosity," Richard answered promptly. "I knew the minute I saw you that we had a lot in common."

"I also have a dog," Jeanne teased. But it was pleasant to have a boy care enough to count ways that they might be alike. If only David. . . . She stopped the thought before it began. "What about your friend? Did he or she stand you up? Should we be getting worried?"

"I signed up for the court alone," Richard confessed. "I was going to ask you to play with me."

"Oh." Somehow, the knowledge that Richard was going out of his way to be with her stunned Jeanne into silence.

"Can you stand another set?" Richard asked. "You don't have to go yet, do you?"

"Not yet," Jeanne answered. And then there was more silence as she realized that Richard was at least interested enough in her to want to spend this time with her. He was the first, and she was amused at the fact that her primary reaction was dismay.

After the game he drove her home and asked for her telephone number. When she gave it to him, he asked, "What else do you like to do? Besides tennis, I mean. What are you interested in?"

"Drama," she answered promptly. "I'm planning to be an actress."

"Would you like to go to see a play this Saturday night?" he asked promptly.

Jeanne was truly startled at the sudden invitation, but she managed to say, "Sure," without showing her surprise.

"Good," Richard said. "It will be the break I need before I begin studying for midterms. I should warn you, I study a lot. I'm a senior and have to get into a good college."

She nodded her head, not quite sure what he meant. Later, when Darla called and she repeated the comment to her, Jeanne said, "I think he was trying to let me down easy. Warn me in advance not to count on him."

"Maybe he just meant what he said. That he has to study a lot," Darla said. "Anyway, do you like him?"

"I like him," Jeanne conceded. She didn't add that her feelings of liking Richard had nothing in common with the love she felt for David.

"So this is a big week," Darla said. "You get to go out on a date with a *senior* in high school. And next week you get the part of Juliet."

"Don't count on it," Jeanne said. "I'm not."

"Everyone's certain you and David will be the leads," Darla said.

"Then he is going to try out?" Jeanne asked.

"I think so. Of course, it's hard to tell now that he and Kathy are fighting."

"Fighting?" How is it that her heart could suddenly begin to beat like a drum just at the mention of David's name?

"Kathy told me they had another big

fight. This time because he wouldn't take her to the basketball game."

"But they made up?"

"I guess so. But I think they're about finished with each other. Seems like they fight a lot."

"They never used to," Jeanne said. She wished she didn't feel so elated at the possibility of her friend losing her boyfriend. It didn't seem very nice. Besides, just because David and Kathy broke up was no real reason to believe that she had a chance.

"Maybe they're bored with each other," Darla said.

"Maybe," Jeanne said. She had long wondered why David wasn't more impatient with Kathy's lack of imagination. David seemed so bright and so nice. . . . "I have to go now," Jeanne said. No matter how much she dreamed of David, she didn't want to fall into the trap of talking about her friend or even of thinking mean thoughts about her.

"Have fun tomorrow night," Darla said.

"What?" Jeanne asked.

"On your date. Have fun."

"Sure," Jeanne answered. Funny how the prospect of a date with Richard had dimmed in importance now that she'd heard the news about Kathy and David.

Chapter 12

Jeanne almost had another fight with Amanda, but this time it was about her date with Richard, because her stepmother fussed and worried so much about what Jeanne was going to wear. Finally, she snapped, "Just relax, Amanda. He's just an ordinary boy and it's just an ordinary date."

Amanda's voice trembled. "I was just trying to help. I only said you might want to dress up a bit more."

"Mom bought this sweater for me." Jeanne glared and pulled the bulky yellow sweater up to her face. She had been thinking of wearing the yellow sweater with her new gray slacks. While that wasn't very dressy, she was very proud of the way she looked in those slacks. Slim hips made quite a difference.

But when Richard picked her up she was wearing a simple mint-green dress. Her auburn hair was freshly washed and set in a fluffy, more elegant style.

"You look pretty tonight," her father said.

Richard didn't say anything about her appearance, but he seemed very pleased to be with her. On the way to the theater he told her about his plans for the future. "I've wanted a degree in engineering ever since I was old enough to figure out I was going to have to work."

"So that's what you study so hard? You want to be an engineer."

"What I study so hard is English and history," Richard said. "I need a straight-A average to get into the university on a full scholarship."

"You must be very smart," Jeanne said.

Richard seemed to enjoy himself at the theater very much. It was a French farce with a lot of romping around the stage and acrobatic fighting with swords. The actress who played the lead not only couldn't act very well, she forgot her lines twice.

Jeanne studied the girl bitterly, knowing well that the only reason she'd been given the part was that she was so pretty. Her small body was perfect for all the scenes where she was tossed from man to man as a part of the farcical fighting.

Jeanne sighed and shifted in her seat jealously. She would never get parts like that, no matter how good she got. And if she dieted down to pure bones, she would outweigh that girl by 20 or 30 pounds. What's more, she was probably taller than half the men on that stage. Life simply wasn't fair.

On the way out of the theater, Richard said, "It was fun, wasn't it?"

"I wish she hadn't forgotten her lines so often," Jeanne said.

"Who?"

"Marciella, the lead."

"Oh, the girl," Richard said, dismissing her immediately. "What I liked best was the way those guys moved. Do you suppose they're good tennis players?"

Jeanne laughed. "Ballet dancers, probably. A lot of actors take ballet to help them with the fight scenes."

"You really know a lot about the theater, don't you? Are you serious about acting?"

"As serious as you are about engineering," Jeanne assured him.

"Will you study drama in college?"

"If I go," Jeanne said. "But I may decide to skip college and start right out on my acting career."

"How can you do that?"

"I might get a place as an apprentice

here at the Old Globe this summer. And that might lead to other things."

"You mean work at the Old Globe as an actress?"

"If I try out as an apprentice and get it, I'll have to do whatever they want me to. That could be building sets or doing walk-ons."

"What do you mean, *if* you try out? If that's what you want, you should go for it."

Jeanne nodded. "You're right. From now on, I'll say, '*When* I try out.' But I can guarantee you they won't give me the lead."

"You'd make a good Marciella," Richard said. "I bet you'd never forget your lines."

Jeanne laughed and bit her tongue to keep from saying anything about how hard it would be to toss her around the stage. If Richard hadn't noticed, there was no sense bringing it to his attention.

Richard didn't suggest stopping for a Coke on the way home, and the conversation seemed to lag as they moved along the darkened streets. Jeanne couldn't think of anything to say, and Richard didn't volunteer anything. When they pulled up to the curb in front of her house, he got out of the car very quickly and walked her to the door. "Thank you," he said, and shook her hand. "I hope we can do this again sometime."

"That would be nice," Jeanne said politely.

"See you on the tennis courts tomorrow?" Richard asked.

"Not for at least three days," Jeanne said. "Tryouts for the school play are on Wednesday and I want to prepare."

Richard nodded and added, "Good luck," before he walked away. He didn't look back in her direction. She was surprised at how disappointed she was that he didn't seem more enthusiastic about the prospect of seeing her again.

She lay awake a long time that night wondering why Richard had lost interest in her so quickly. Was it because of her height? When they'd first met she'd been wearing shorts and she probably looked closer to normal in tennis shoes. Even in heels, she was a bit shorter than he, but maybe he didn't like going out with a girl who was close to six feet tall.

She tried to turn her thoughts to other things, but the minute she stopped worrying about her date with Richard, she started worrying about trying out for the part of Juliet.

The idea of playing opposite David was simply much too good to believe. She tried to see herself in a slim white satin dress and a small beaded cap. She tried to see herself leaning over the balcony and calling down into the shadows where Romeo stood. But she couldn't.

She beat her pillow into a fluffier shape and turned on to her side. One by one, she let go of things that were outside her ability to change, and finally she fell asleep.

Amanda seemed more disappointed that her date was a dud than she was. "How can you tell he didn't like you?" Amanda demanded.

"Because he shook my hand," Jeanne said as she chewed slowly on a dry piece of toast. One thing all this dieting had taught her was that the slower she ate, the fuller she felt. Not that she ever really felt full anymore, anyway. She looked enviously at the bacon, eggs, toast, and marmalade on Hank's plate, and tugged at her toast.

This morning the scale had been stuck on the same spot that it had been on for the last week. No matter what she ate, she couldn't seem to budge that needle. She knew that she was in one of those periods that Anna Marie called a plateau, and that if she just kept on the program she would eventually break out of the stuck place. But it was certainly discouraging, especially since she'd decided to eat even less than allowed on the program. It never occurred to her that that was one of the reasons she was so hungry and discouraged.

She had hoped to weigh 130 pounds when she tried out for Juliet, but she'd been stuck at 145 for ten days. There was no way she'd come close to her original goal, but she would love to be below 140. How could you feel like a Shakespearean heroine with a number like 145 staring at you every morning?

Jeanne swallowed the last of her toast. Now there would be a grapefruit half and then four hours of starvation until lunch. Then she might splurge and have a peach with her dish of cottage cheese. She should have eaten more, but she was desperate.

At school, Darla was almost as disappointed as Amanda had been. "You mean he went to all that trouble to meet you at the tennis court, and then he took you to that expensive play and he didn't even try to kiss you?"

"That's right," Jeanne said.

"What happened?"

"Nothing, I told you that."

"Did you make a lot of jokes?" Darla demanded.

"Just the usual number." Jeanne laughed and admitted, "I did quote a little poetry at one point."

"In one of your voices, probably," Darla said. "You can't act that way with boys and have them take you seriously."

"Probably not," Jeanne agreed. "Did you get your history done?" She had honestly lost interest in hashing over her date with Richard.

"No," Darla said. "At least I didn't get all my essay questions done. I need help on six and eighteen."

They opened their notebooks and began to compare short essays, but before they got very far at all, Kathy Murdock joined them. It was unusual for Kathy to join them early in the morning in the library, and Jeanne knew the minute she sat down beside them that something exciting had happened.

Kathy opened the conversation with, "I had the best weekend of my life. A guy my brother knows called me and we went sightseeing in Los Angeles two days in a row. We saw everything. We went to that Chinese theater and walked up and down Sunset Boulevard. And we took a tour of Universal Studios. Kyle is so handsome that a lady thought he was a movie star. He's moving out here next month."

"What happened to David?" Jeanne asked. She noticed that the words came out very slowly and that her mouth seemed to be abnormally dry, as though she were talking with a tongue made of cotton.

"David?" Kathy shrugged. "That's all over."

"Does David know that?" Jeanne asked. She could barely get the words out.

"I don't know and I don't care what David knows," Kathy said. "His name is Kyle and he's from Connecticut. My brother met him when he visited my uncle last year, and so Kyle just called up on Friday night and asked if Bob was home. I said Bob was living in Santa Cruz now, but we'd be glad to have him come over anyway. You see, I already knew what Kyle looked like because Bob showed me his picture a long time ago. And you know what? He said he only called because Bob had showed him a picture of me. He knew Bob was in Santa Cruz all along. Isn't that funny?"

"What did David say about Kyle?" Jeanne asked. She was amazed at how hurt she was for David and how angry she felt at Kathy for causing him pain. She had always known that Kathy was a foolish girl who didn't appreciate what she had. Now it appeared that she was also heartless.

"Why are you so worried about David?" Kathy asked.

"He's my friend," Jeanne said.

"I thought *I* was your friend."

"You are." Jeanne wondered how true that really was. Would Kathy be her friend if it weren't for David?

"Then if you're my friend, you'll loan me your history questions," Kathy said and laughed. "I had such a great weekend that I didn't have time to do my homework. I told Kyle that from now on he was going to have to give me a little time to myself. But he said now that he's found me, he's not going to take a chance on losing me. Isn't that sweet?"

"That's sweet," Jeanne said. But the words were flat and disinterested. The truth of the matter was that she didn't care a thing about Kathy's new love. All she really cared about was the fact that now that Kathy and David were finished, there might be a slight possibility of a chance for her.

She closed her eyes and willed herself to see herself on stage in a white satin dress with a beaded cap. Then she placed David on that stage beside her and heard him call her name. "Juliet, sweet Juliet."

"What are you doing?" Kathy demanded. "Why are your eyes shut?"

"I'm daydreaming," Jeanne admitted, and then laughed.

Kathy shook her head and said, "You are weird. Give me those history questions."

Chapter 13

On the morning of the tryouts, Jeanne stepped on the scale and discovered that she'd lost another five pounds. She stared down at the number 140 and felt joy rise up from her toes and spread throughout her entire body. For the first time in her life, she actually felt almost slender.

She wore a soft white cotton skirt and matching silk blouse to school, carefully chosen to represent Juliet's costume. With her off-white stockings and shoes, she looked quite theatrical. She brushed her thick auburn hair into a soft page boy, curling it with Amanda's curling iron into waves. For makeup, she used only some pink blusher and a sharper pink lipstick.

She passed David in the halls three times that day and each time she exchanged some sort of greeting with him. The last time she asked, "Nervous?"

"Not really," he said. "I only said I'd try out for Romeo to get a better grade in drama. I need an A."

"You'll get the part," Jeanne volunteered. She hoped that he would return her assurances, but he only shrugged and smiled.

Jeanne was so nervous at lunch that it was easy for her not to eat. She sat with Darla and Kathy, sipping orange juice while they devoured hamburgers with French fries and talked about school and boys. Kathy was still full of excitement over her new boyfriend, but she did find enough curiosity to ask Jeanne, "You never said how your date turned out. Did you like him?"

"Who?"

"Your date — Robert?"

"Richard," Jeanne corrected. "Yes. He was nice."

"Has he called you again?"

"No." From the corner of her eye, Jeanne could see David standing by the cashier. He was holding his tray and obviously looking for someone to sit beside. Her heart began to thump at the possibility that he would choose their table. Perhaps he would sit with them and ignore Kathy. Maybe he would speak only to her. Maybe he would smile and say something like, "As long as we're going to be co-stars, we might as well lunch together." Maybe. . . . Jeanne's dreams trailed off as David sat down beside Marybeth Gibbons.

She pushed the orange juice away, feeling slightly sick to her stomach. Why did David want a beautiful girl like Marybeth or a cute girl like Kathy when he could have a real live person like her? Maybe David wasn't as nice and smart as he seemed. Maybe David was really an idiot who just happened to make good grades, be handsome, polite, and well-liked by everyone.

"Who do you think will get Juliet?" Kathy asked. "Marybeth or Alice?"

"I think Jeanne will," Darla said, and frowned at Kathy in warning.

Kathy opened her mouth and closed it, then said, "Well, what about Romeo?"

"David," Jeanne and Darla both said.

Kathy shook her head. "I don't think so. I think Murphy will give it to Jason Morales."

"Why would he do that?" Jeanne demanded. "Jason Morales can't even remember his lines half the time."

"I just think Jason looks like Romeo. David is too blond."

"How do you know Romeo isn't blond?" Jeanne asked.

"He's Italian," Kathy insisted. "Jason looks more Italian."

"But you think he'll pick a blond to play Juliet," Jeanne reminded her. "Isn't Juliet Italian, too?"

"That doesn't matter," Kathy said. "Heroines are always blond."

"Let's change the subject," Darla said. "We don't want to bring Jeanne bad luck by talking about it on the day of the try-outs."

"You can't bring me bad luck," Jeanne said. "I make my own luck."

Despite her brave words, Jeanne was nervous as she stood in the wings and watched the other actors try out for the parts of Romeo and Juliet. Since there were only three boys trying out — Jason Morales, David Green, and Nick Williams — they rotated the scene, each one playing against three actresses.

Jeanne was the second Juliet and she didn't know whether that was a good or bad sign, but it meant that she had a chance to unleash her intense emotions very early and almost relax as she watched the others.

At first she was disappointed that she had to play the scene against Nick Williams, but then she decided it was best.

Nick was the tallest of the boys and she would look smaller opposite him than with David or Jason. And she wasn't in love with Nick, so she could concentrate on her acting without letting any other nervousness interfere.

She put everything she had into the part, remembering every trick she'd ever read or learned. She walked onto the stage with her hands held upward to give herself an eager appearance. She put a musical lilt in her voice. She kept her body turned to the side of the stage so that she would look as thin as possible.

When she finished, she knew she'd done the very best job she possibly could as Juliet. As she walked off the stage, two of the other girls nodded and smiled, indicating that they thought she was wonderful. And David whispered, "You were great."

His breath brushed the nape of her neck, sending chills down her spine. She turned and said, "You will be, too."

This time he smiled at her and looked directly into her eyes as he said, "No. I mean you were really great. As good as any professional."

She smiled gratefully at him. No matter what else happened that day, she would have his praise to warm her and to remind her that she had truly done her best.

"Thanks," she whispered, and sat down on a stool to watch the other Juliets with a hopeful heart.

She was the best Juliet. That was clear. Marybeth looked good but her voice was so high it was almost a whine. None of the others was any serious competition. As she watched one girl after another go onto the stage, her hopes climbed. There was no way that anyone could deny that she had been the best Juliet. She was sure of that.

While her hopes climbed for herself, they dropped for David. When it was his first turn to play Romeo opposite Marybeth, they looked so good together that it was hard to understand how bad they both were. Marybeth's high voice seemed to push her lines onto the stage breathlessly, and David seemed to rush his lines back. The timing was all wrong and David looked very nervous.

The second time he played Romeo, it was opposite a small, dark girl named Mandy, and he did better. Though it pained her to admit, he still wasn't very good, but he did seem less nervous. His third time on the stage, he actually forgot his lines and Jeanne's heart sank.

By the end of the tryouts, she was certain that Jason Morales would get the part instead of David. Not only did Jason look like

Romeo, but he was really quite good. And the fact that Jason was certain to get the part was bad news for her because he was the shortest of the three boys. She wasn't certain, but she believed she might be taller than he was. She tried her best to believe that Mr. Murphy wouldn't make a decision based on something as shallow as how tall she was. Surely he would pick the best actress for the role.

When everyone had had a chance to try out, Jeanne sat quietly in a chair, waiting for Mr. Murphy to announce his decision. She forced herself to keep her hands limp in her lap and to show absolutely none of the nervousness she felt. She forced herself to hope for the best. She was a good actress and she deserved to win.

She was too good an actress to let her disappointment show when Mr. Murphy said, "Romeo will be Jason Morales and Juliet will be Marybeth Gibbons." Jeanne clapped politely and waited as Mr. Murphy went on. "Jeanne Lee will play the nurse and David Green will be Mercutio."

There were a few minutes of confusion as everyone talked about the news. David pointedly came over to her. "You were ripped off, you know."

"I know." She felt more anger than pain,

though she knew the pain would come in time.

"Can I walk you home?" David asked.

"I want to talk to Mr. Murphy," Jeanne said. Somewhere in the back of her mind, she knew she should have been elated at David's offer, but all she cared about was confronting the drama teacher. He wasn't fair and she intended to tell him so.

"It won't do any good," David said softly. "Come on, I'll take you home."

"After I talk with him," Jeanne said. She wondered where she got the strength to put David behind her acting. She would have said that she would give up anything to be with David, but that didn't seem to be true.

Eventually most of the others drifted away. Jeanne stepped in front of Mr. Murphy and asked in a tight, angry voice, "Why didn't I get Juliet? Wasn't I the best actress?"

"You're not right for the part."

"I'm thinner now. Did you even look at me? Do you think it's fair to turn me down just because I'm tall?"

"I didn't turn you down just because you're tall," Mr. Murphy answered. "I didn't turn you down at all. I gave you the best part in the play."

"The nurse?"

"That's right, the nurse. With your comic ability, you can keep the story alive. Cheer up, Jeanne. You've got the best part."

"No, I haven't," she said quietly. "You gave the best part to a girl who can't act, but who's small and pretty."

Mr. Murphy sighed and turned his eyes heavenward, then he raised his arms to the ceiling and implored the stagelighting, "Do you see what I have to put up with? Nerves. And adolescent jitters."

"I was the best," Jeanne said stubbornly.

"Listen to me, Jeanne. If you're going to make it in the theater, you're going to have to learn to take your lumps. You didn't get Juliet. So what? Do you think you're going to get every part you try out for? I thought you were a trooper."

"I just want you to admit the truth," Jeanne said. She was beginning to feel very foolish. What good was any of this doing? He wouldn't take the part away from Marybeth and hand it to her. And Mr. Murphy never admitted he was wrong or unjust.

She felt like she wanted to take him and shake him until he admitted he'd been unfair.

"Why didn't you give me Juliet?" she asked again.

"Because I need you as nurse," Mr. Murphy answered, then he packed up his briefcase and started for the door. He did stop long enough to ask, "Want a ride home?"

"No."

"Jeanne?"

"What." The tears were coming now and she didn't even bother to try and hide them.

"Remember, you're a trooper. Right?" When Jeanne didn't answer, he shrugged and headed for the door. Then he turned and asked again, "Sure you don't want a ride? It's dark out."

"No, I'll walk"

"You have a gift for comedy," he began, but when Jeanne shook her head in denial, he added, "I'll let you nurse your own wounds tonight. See you at rehearsal tomorrow."

Jeanne didn't answer. She was trying not to cry, but she was so blinded by tears by the time she walked out of the school building that it took her a minute to recognize who was calling to her. "Jeanne."

Jeanne saw that it was David. She found a Kleenex in her purse and blew her nose, then she wiped her eyes and said, "I guess you think it's silly to cry over a part in a play."

"No," David said. "I can see why you're

disappointed. You deserved the part because you were best."

"Thank you."

"Murphy's weird," David said. "He's kind of mean in a funny way. What did he say when you asked him why he ripped you off?"

"He said he needed me as the nurse. That I had a comic talent."

"Oh." David thought that one over for a while and then he said, "You will be good as the nurse. You'd be good as anything."

Then he patted her on the arm and asked, "Want to stop and have an ice cream or something?"

"Sure, why not?" Jeanne said. Who was she to turn down an invitation to be with the man of her dreams just because it involved a few thousand calories?

"Maybe you should have a double scoop," David said. "You look awful thin these days."

Jeanne laughed and said. "Okay. I'll have a double scoop. Half butter almond and half chocolate fudge ripple. Drown my sorrows in sugar."

Chapter 14

Everyone was so nice to Jeanne about losing the part that she began to feel a little shy. At the same time she was pleased by all the attention. Not only did David buy her an ice-cream cone and take her home, but when she got there, Amanda hugged her and said, "We heard the news. Your friend Marybeth called to apologize, and she told us."

"Marybeth Gibbons?"

"Yes, she wants you to call her. Jeanne, she feels terrible. She says she was certain you would get the part and she thinks you were cheated. She even offered to drop out."

"You're kidding!"

"I told her you wouldn't want her to do that, of course. But do call her."

"I'll talk to her tomorrow," Jeanne said. Though she was surprised that Marybeth had called, she wasn't sorry that Amanda had been able to talk her out of giving up the part. Tomorrow would be soon enough to congratulate Marybeth.

The phone rang and it was Darla, who spent thirty minutes talking about how unfair Mr. Murphy was. Then Kathy called and after that, two other girls who had also tried out for Juliet. Everyone agreed that Jeanne should have had the part. At eight-thirty, Jeanne joined her family in the living room and asked, "Who was it that said, 'I'd rather be right than President'?"

"Calvin Coolidge," Hank said.

"Couldn't be. He was President," her father said. "It was probably someone like Al Smith. Why do you ask?"

"I'm thinking of writing my memoirs. I'll call them 'I'd Rather Be Right for the Part Than Juliet.'"

"I'm glad to see you're taking this so well," her father said. "After all, it's only the beginning of your career. When you're a successful actress, you'll look back on this and laugh."

Jeanne actually found the courage to smile at her father as she said, "You're right." It was the first time he'd ever referred to her acting career as anything but a high school dream, and she decided to pursue her advantage. "I want to try out to be an apprentice at the Old Globe this summer. I'll have to have your permission and I suppose I'll have to have a ride to get there."

"I don't know," her father said doubtfully.

"If Jeanne is accepted, I'll be happy to drive her," Amanda intercepted quickly. "She ought to be encouraged."

"Thanks, Amanda." The telephone rang before she could say more, but she was truly grateful for her stepmother's support.

This time it was Richard, who asked, "Want to play tennis tomorrow?"

"I can't," Jeanne said. "In fact, I can't play tennis for at least five weeks. I'm in the class play and our drama coach says we all have to be at rehearsal every night."

"Congratulations. Do I call you Juliet now?"

Jeanne felt tears rush to her eyes, but she kept her voice level and cheerful as she said, "No, and don't you dare call me Nurse, either. I didn't get Juliet, but I got the second lead. The comic one."

"You're good at comedy, aren't you?"

"So they say." Jeanne wondered if all "big" girls were supposed to be good at comedy. Wasn't it always true that people expected fat people to be jolly? Maybe she wasn't any better at comedy than anyone else. Maybe she was just bigger than the other girls, so she got the funny part.

"I'm working this weekend," Richard said. "But I'll call you in a week or two and maybe we can go to the movies or something. Okay?"

"Okay." It was good to know that Richard was interested enough in her to call back. It made her feel like less of a loser.

She dressed carefully for school the next day, wearing her prettiest pink sweater and gray skirt. She curled her hair and spent some time putting on makeup. Even if she was doomed to the dumb parts, she was determined not to let it show. And she was gratified to see that her weight was still at 140. That was one thing Mr. Murphy couldn't take away from her — her new figure.

David was friendly, but not a bit friendlier than he'd been before the tryouts. Though she stopped twice in the halls to talk to him, he brushed aside her thanks for the ice cream with a quick shrug. And that night after rehearsals, he didn't offer to walk her home again.

Life took on a pattern the next few weeks that was both pleasant and busy. To her dismay, Jeanne found she enjoyed the part of the nurse. There was something about the loud, swaggering, rotund character that was endearing. As she practiced, she got so far into the part that she discovered that she was actually growing fond of Marybeth.

Marybeth was a pretty, sweet girl who was trying her best to play Juliet with some emotion, but she was no actress. Sometimes when Jeanne was playing a scene with her, she felt as though she were on the stage all alone. As the days wore on, Mr. Murphy seemed to give up totally on Marybeth and concentrate all his energies on Jeanne and Jason Morales.

Richard called twice while she was rehearsing, and she went to the movies with him one night.

Jeanne enjoyed Richard's company more than she'd expected.

"So did he kiss you this time?" Darla demanded the next day.

"No," Jeanne said.

"I hope you didn't tell too many jokes," Darla said.

"How many is too many?" Jeanne was smiling now, remembering how he had laughed at her imitation of Mr. Murphy doing Juliet's lines. "He laughed in the right places."

"You've got to get over being the comedienne if you want to be taken seriously by boys," Darla said. "I've told you that a million times."

"More like ten million," Jeanne teased. For the first time it occurred to her that Darla had a lot of advice, but she hadn't had much more experience. She thought about her dates with Richard and shook her head. No. Richard liked her just the way she was. He didn't want her to go around with a sweet little smile on her face and nothing between her ears. Richard liked her because she was sharp and funny.

"When Kyle gets back we can double-date," Kathy offered. There was a wistfulness in her voice that told Jeanne she was beginning to wonder exactly when Kyle would be moving out here.

"When is he coming out?" Darla asked. "I thought it was only supposed to be two weeks."

"It's his father's transfer," Kathy explained. "It was supposed to come through a month ago, but it hasn't."

"Do you think he might not move here?" Jeanne asked. The idea of Kathy without a permanent boyfriend bothered her more than she liked to admit. Though David didn't seem very interested in any girl at the moment, Jeanne still hoped she might someday capture his interest. If Kathy was to suddenly change her mind. . . . Jeanne was relieved by Kathy's answer.

"I know it's just a question of time. It's just not going as fast as they'd hoped. But Kyle is still calling me just about every night. I can hardly wait for him to get here. You'll like him, Jeanne."

"I'm sure I will." Why not? She liked Kathy's old boyfriend more than any boy she'd ever met. Working with David on the play had confirmed the fact that he was a nice person. And he was so good-looking. There were times, when David stood on the stage and Jeanne looked at him, that she thought he was handsome enough to be a movie star. But of course David wanted to be an airline pilot, not a movie star.

Jeanne smiled at the thought. She hoped that David was better at piloting jets than he was in the role of Mercutio.

"What are you laughing at?" Darla asked.

"Nothing. I was just thinking about Mr. Murphy's latest thing. Now he wants us to pack supper in case we have to work until midnight."

"You're kidding!"

"We haven't actually worked past seven yet, but he keeps threatening. To tell you the truth, I think it's a toss-up whether he gets this play on the stage or we call the orderlies in the white coats. I can see Murphy sitting in his straitjacket shouting Juliet's lines at the top of his voice."

"Is he still picking on Marybeth?" Darla asked.

"Not as much," Jeanne admitted. "I think he's sort of given up."

"He should have given you the part," Darla said. "Everyone says so."

"I hope that hasn't made it harder for Marybeth. I'd feel really guilty."

"For being better than her?" Kathy asked.

"She's had a hard time and she's a nice girl."

When both Darla and Kathy looked doubtful, Jeanne went on. "I've gone out for pizza with some of the cast twice. Both times Marybeth was there, and she is really nice. You know, I think it's hard to be as beautiful as Marybeth. No one really sees you."

"I feel so sorry for *poooor* Marybeth," Kathy said mockingly. "Does David go for pizza with you?"

There it was, the sharp stab of fear right in her solar plexis. "Yes, but you know David. He's nice to everyone, including Marybeth. I think Jason has a thing for her, but I can't tell for sure."

"Sounds kind of like fun," Kathy said and yawned. "Maybe I should have tried out for a part."

"One more week and it will all be over," Jeanne said. She stood up, suddenly needing to get away from them. "Then all I'll have to do is catch up on five weeks of homework so I don't flunk my sophomore year." Then she laughed as she walked away and tossed her last comment over her shoulder. "Then again, if I flunk out, I can try out for the lead in the class play again. Maybe the next time Murphy will have learned his lesson and give it to me."

During that last week of rehearsal, Mr. Murphy made it clear that he was sorry he'd chosen Marybeth, and that he had decided to solve her acting problems by basically ignoring her, and turning the play into a cross between a comedy and a battle. He gave more and more emphasis to the fighting scenes and encouraged Jeanne to be rowdier and rowdier in her part. While she enjoyed the permission to upstage everyone, she felt sorry for the actors with the straight parts.

Mr. Murphy also cut a lot of Juliet's scenes because Marybeth still was having trouble with her lines. She knew them well enough, but she'd deliver them, and then Mr. Murphy would yell some direction at her, telling her to be sweeter or slower or stronger. Marybeth would look at him, blink her eyes, and repeat the lines with exactly the same inflection. If he yelled at her a second time, she would forget them.

David wasn't much stronger as an actor than Marybeth, but he didn't have a lead part so it didn't matter much. And David honestly didn't seem to mind that he wasn't very good. He repeated his lines over and over, but Jeanne knew he never once put his whole heart into trying.

Some of the cast went out for pizza together every night that last week. Jeanne always went along because she got to sit next to David in his car. By Wednesday, when Jeanne got on the scale, she had gained five pounds. She groaned and made a face at herself in the mirror, saying aloud, "Once this play is over, you go back to starving, kiddo."

Having promised herself to diet after the weekend of the play, she ate a third slice of pizza that evening. David smiled at her and said, "You must be hungry. I've never see you eat much except salad."

"I've been eating pizza every night this week," she said. "Same as you."

"One slice with a salad," he said.

Her heart fluttered with hope. If David

noticed what she ate, then he must be noticing her. She smiled and agreed sweetly. "All the energy I put out on the stage makes me hungry, I guess."

"You're good," he said. "I can't get over how good you are."

"Thank you." She put the pizza slice down and said, "I guess I'm not as hungry as I thought." If David was even remotely interested in her, she wasn't going to spoil it by getting fat.

As the others laughed and talked, Jeanne sat quietly, watching David out of the corner of her eye. He had the nicest profile she'd ever seen. His nose was straight and just the right size. Even his ears were handsome, she decided, and she loved the way his blond hair curled just slightly around the edge of his face. She wondered what it would be like to be kissed by David, and the idea brought color to her cheeks.

David, who had just turned sixteen and gotten his driver's license, had been allowed to use his mother's car during most of the rehearsals. He drove a carload of kids home and as usual, she sat in front. This evening, he changed his route so she would be the last one out. She hoped that was a good omen. After they dropped off Jason and they were alone, David asked,

"What were you thinking about? Back there in the restaurant? I saw you looking at me."

Jeanne flushed in the darkness. What could she say? Should she tell David the truth? That she was thinking about how much she liked him? She couldn't. "My friend Lori. You remember her? I was thinking about Lori."

"Then why were you looking at me?"

Jeanne laughed, hoping he would think it was amusement, not nervousness, that caused the merriment. "Lori used to have this big crush on you. From the second grade on. You were sort of a joke."

"A joke."

"I don't mean you were a *joke*. The joke was that Lori was madly in love with you and you never even noticed her. So sometimes I look at you and I think how great it would be if Lori were here. She would have been a good Juliet."

"She had brown hair? A thin girl?"

"Her hair was really more blonde than brown. She moved away. I still miss her and sometimes when I'm with you, I get homesick for Lori."

"Oh." David pulled up in front of her door and she couldn't wait to get out of the car. She was so embarrassed that she promised herself she would never look at any boy again!

"Do you write to Lori?" David asked.

"Sometimes. She doesn't write back very often."

"Next time you write, tell her I said hello."

"I will," Jeanne said. Once again, she was struck by how nice David was. A lot of boys would have laughed or said something stupid, but not David. He said just the right thing. She opened the car door and said, "See you tomorrow."

"Dress rehearsal at two. First performance at eight," David reminded her.

"Second performance on Saturday and it's all over." The idea made her sad. There was no reason to believe she'd spend any time at all with David after that.

Chapter 15

They performed their dress rehearsal for the freshmen who had afternoon English classes. While the audience was very small, it was large enough to give the director and actors some idea of the reaction they could expect in the two final performances.

Jeanne had to admit that Mr. Murphy had been right about cutting Juliet's lines and playing up the action. The audience obviously loved all the sword play, and every time Jeanne came onstage they broke into spontaneous applause.

Mr. Murphy seemed pleased enough. After it was over, he made a few fast suggestions and then sent them all home to relax. "Don't even think about the play until you get back here at a quarter to seven," he advised.

Most of the kids were startled by Murphy's abrupt dismissal, and they clustered in small bands outside the stage door. Finally, Jason Morales said, "Let's not go home. Let's go eat one last pizza. For old time's sake."

There was laughter and quick agreement and they piled into David's car. Another two carloads of actors followed and they invaded Philippe's Pizza at four-thirty in the afternoon. When they got there, Marybeth said, "I'm too nervous to eat."

"Can't be nervous," Jason reminded her. "Mr. Murphy said we weren't to even think about the play."

"How are we going to spend two more hours together and *not* talk about the play?" Marybeth asked. "It doesn't make sense."

"We could tell each other the story of our lives," Jeanne suggested.

"I haven't had a life," Marybeth said. "I'm only fifteen years old."

Some of the others laughed, but Jeanne could see that Marybeth hadn't meant to be funny. She was really upset. Jeanne said, "Tell you what, Marybeth, you don't have to do anything but drink a 7-Up or something. I'll tell you the story of my life. It's really quite amusing."

She switched to a British accent and went into one of her routines. "My name is Lady Pamela Jeanne Twitter Townsand and I was born in a castle. Not a large castle, mind you. Just a teeny weeny castle in the remote English countryside. My father, dear Papa, was never good with money, gambled away the castle when I was only a child, and I had to go on the stage. Of course, there aren't many parts for ladies so I became a cowgirl impersonator. . . ."

They were all laughing, including Marybeth, when the waitress came to the table. As they ordered, each of them tried to do an accent of their own. Jason ordered his pizza in French and David tried German. Even Marybeth managed a slight Southern drawl.

"How do you do it?" Jason asked Jeanne. "How come you're so good with voices?"

"I've seen a lot of theater and I listen to radio plays. Public broadcasting does old ones, you know. But mostly it's just having a good ear and practicing."

"It helps to have talent," David said. He was smiling directly at her and Jeanne flushed with pleasure. David did like her, she was sure of that! Now if she could only find some way to turn that liking into an interest that was more romantic.

At exactly the same time the pizza arrived, Darla and Kathy walked into the pizza parlor. Kathy's face lit up and she called, "Hi, Jeanne."

Reluctantly, Jeanne asked them over and someone invited them to sit down. All that was unavoidable, but when Kathy pushed her chair between Jeanne and David, it was as if she had pushed a knife directly into Jeanne's heart. Within three minutes, it was clear to everyone that Kathy was trying to make up with David.

Kathy laughed a little too much and seemed a bit nervous, but she went directly to the point. As she bit into a slice of the pizza she said softly, "I'll be glad when this old play is finished. I haven't seen nearly enough of Jeanne." Then she turned her head and smiled directly at David and said, "And I miss you."

Jeanne felt herself going numb all over. She chewed on the pizza even though it had turned to cardboard in her mouth. And she couldn't hear anything anyone was saying except for the low whispers that were going on between Kathy and David. Funny how you could be turned to stone and still feel so terrible.

They sat as a group for two hours, laughing and talking and having a great time. Jeanne used all her skill as an actress to cover the torment she was going through. She was the life of the party while David and Kathy renewed their interest in each other.

At six-fifteen, they all put money on the table to cover the check and started back to the cars. Kathy said, "I wonder if Mr. Murphy would mind if Darla and I came in early."

"What would you do?" Jeanne managed to ask. She knew it wasn't fair to hate Kathy. It wasn't as if Kathy was actually taking David away from her. David had never been Jeanne's and he wasn't an object to take, anyway. But at that moment, she could have cheerfully killed Kathy Murdock.

"I could help with the costumes," Kathy said brightly. Then she turned again to David and asked, "Do you have room for us in your car?"

So Jeanne rode back crushed against the door of the car while Kathy cuddled in the middle, leaning as close to David as she possibly could. At that moment, Jeanne hated herself for being so big. If she'd been as slim as Marybeth, she could have sat in the backseat with Jason, Tim, and Mike. But she wasn't slim and she wasn't beautiful. She was just Jeanne.

She was miserable as she put on her makeup in the dressing room. It was hard not to feel sorry for herself as she applied the bright red rouge to her cheeks and padded the front of her blouse with pillows to make herself look comical. And the bright red wig that Mr. Murphy was having her wear looked like it came off Bozo the Clown.

When she finished with all her makeup, she sat and stared at herself in the mirror, wishing the reflection that stared back at her were a slim blonde in a satin dress with a beaded skull cap. The difference between what she wished she saw and what she actually did see made her laugh out loud.

"How can you laugh?" Marybeth asked. "Aren't you nervous?"

"Not very," Jeanne admitted. "There's nothing to be nervous about."

"That's easy for you to say," Marybeth said. "You've got talent." She was clearly envious.

Jeanne turned to face Marybeth and said softly, "You've got a lot going for you, too. I envy your beauty, you know."

Marybeth shrugged. "I know I got this part because of the way I look, but you're pretty, too, and you don't let that stop you from being yourself. I mean, you're talented and you're smart and you're pretty. Everyone likes you. You're special and I'm . . . I'm. . . ." There were tears in Marybeth's voice as it trailed off.

"You're beautiful," Jeanne said. She

couldn't think of anything else to say and she was sorry she couldn't honestly add those other things.

"There are lots of times I've wished I wasn't. People act different around me and I know it's because of the way I look. No one really knows me and sometimes I feel like I don't know myself. I don't even know why I tried out for this part."

Jeanne laughed and shook her head. "A stranger in a strange land. That's what I call that feeling. Like there's someone inside you who no one knows yet, but who is struggling to come out. Right?"

"Right."

"They say the best thing about being a teenager is that you've got lots of time," Jeanne said. "Time to figure it all out — even who you are."

Marybeth managed a small smile and then said, "Well, I know who I'm not. I'm not an actress. I promise you that I'll never set foot on a stage again when we finish this play."

Jeanne laughed. "That's it! If you're never going to be an actress and you know it, there's nothing to be nervous about. What does it matter if you flub the lines? You don't want to be an actress, anyway."

Marybeth's face was pale and she was biting her lip. "I'm scared, Jeanne. I wish

I were brave like you. What if I faint?"

"You won't faint," Jeanne promised her. "And if you do, I'll catch you. What are friends for?"

Marybeth managed another small smile and then it was time for her to take her place backstage. Jeanne whispered, "You'll be the best Juliet you can be and after the play, you'll be Marybeth. Nothing to worry about."

When Marybeth left, Jeanne turned and looked in the mirror again. Only this time she saw herself through Marybeth's eyes. In a way, she'd never really looked at herself as someone others might be jealous of, but she supposed that Marybeth was right. She had a lot.

Yes, that was herself staring back at her from behind the nurse's makeup, and she was all those things that Marybeth said she was. She smiled and said aloud, "Okay, kiddo, time to start counting your blessings. Now get out there and give it all you've got."

Chapter 16

Her mother flew in on Saturday morning and called Jeanne from a friend's apartment. Jeanne was surprised, but pleased. "I couldn't miss seeing your debut in the theater. In fact, I tried hard to get here for your very first performance. How was last night?"

"It was perfect," Jeanne said in a laughing voice. "There were a couple of times when I had to brace poor Juliet up, she was so nervous, but I was just marvelous."

"I'm sure you were. And you'll be even better tonight. I'm so glad I worked it out to get here." She paused and added, "I fly back early tomorrow morning because I have an appointment at noon. Hope you're not too disappointed. It isn't much time, but we can spend a couple of hours together this afternoon. Or after the play."

"Sure." Jeanne was busy unscrambling

her day to mentally make room for her mother. She was supposed to meet Richard for tennis at two but she would have to break that. And she could skip the cast party, which was going to be a drag, anyway. She didn't really want to spend the whole evening trying to avoid watching Kathy and David act like a couple of cooing lovebirds.

"Can you get me a ticket for tonight?" her mother asked.

"Yes. But I'm not sure you'll be able to sit with Amanda and Daddy unless I can get Hank to change seats."

"I'd just as soon sit alone," her mother said. "We can save the big reconciliation scene for your wedding."

Jeanne laughed. "How about if I fix you up with a nice young man I know? My friend Richard asked me to get him a ticket, so I'll get two. Just don't flirt with him. He's my best bet at the moment."

"You've got a boyfriend?"

"Not exactly. More like a friend who happens to be a boy." She added, "The one I wanted got away."

"Doesn't sound as if it's breaking your heart."

"No. I'm my mother's daughter. My heart bounces back." She only wished that were true.

They arranged to meet for lunch and she called Richard. He seemed very happy to be asked to sit with her mother, and offered, "I could pick you both up early and drop you off at the school. Then we could all get a hamburger or something."

"Thanks," she said, "I think that might work out really well. You know something — you're nice."

"I was hoping you'd notice," Richard said in a laughing voice and hung up the telephone.

Jeanne sat and stared at the telephone for a moment, thinking to herself, As long as I'm counting my blessings, maybe I ought to count Richard.

She enjoyed every minute of her time on the stage that evening. When the play was over, she got three curtain calls all by herself, and Mr. Murphy gave her a bouquet of roses that was just as large as the one he gave Marybeth. Then he kissed them both on the cheek and made a speech to the audience about his two lovely and talented actresses.

Afterward, Richard and her mother came backstage to tell her how good she was. Amanda, Hank, and her father followed right behind them. They all spoke politely to each other, and her mother, father, and

Amanda congratulated each other on their talented daughter as Jeanne wiped off her makeup.

By the time she finished, most of the other kids were in their street clothes and they began to leave the backstage area. Jason was the first one who stopped to say hello, and he asked, "You coming to the cast party, Jeanne?"

"Can't," Jeanne answered.

"What a handsome young man he is," Amanda said.

Her mother whispered, "Is that the one who got away?"

Jeanne shook her head and whispered back. "You may meet him. David is his name."

"I like Richard," her mother whispered.

"So do I," she whispered back. But even as she said it, she was aware of a sadness tickling the back of her mind. She wasn't sure she had ever exactly *liked* David — the feelings she'd felt had been too intense for that label. And though she'd resigned herself to living a good life without him, she knew Richard would never be the boy who filled his place.

Marybeth came by and Jeanne introduced her.

"I never would have made it through the play except for Jeanne," Marybeth said before leaving. "See you at the party."

Jeanne didn't answer because Kathy and David were standing there, waiting to congratulate her. She wasn't sure whether or not her mother figured out that David was the love she'd lost, but it wasn't important now. She knew David had never really been hers to lose.

Then Mr. Murphy came by and told everyone how pleased he was with Jeanne's performance.

Then, suddenly, backstage was almost deserted except for her family, and Jeanne realized it was time to go home. She cleared her throat. "Why don't we *all* go out for some ice cream?" She didn't want to be put in the awkward position of having to choose between her parents.

"No," her mother said. "I think you and Richard should go to the cast party. Let the old folks entertain themselves."

"I've barely seen you," Jeanne protested.

"You can fly up next weekend," her mother offered. "But I don't want you to skip your party, and neither do Amanda and your father." She looked at them for confirmation and they nodded agreement.

In the end, the cast party wasn't nearly as bad as Jeanne had imagined. Even though Kathy and David sat in the corner and held hands, she had a great time talking and laughing with the others.

Richard seemed slightly out of place, but he was a good sport, laughing at all their jokes and appearing to have a pretty good time. She was glad he'd come.

Having a high school senior as an escort gave her some extra prestige with the others that helped numb the pain of knowing that she would never attract David. She managed to have a perfectly good time as long as she kept her eyes from the corner where he and Kathy sat holding hands and glowing with happiness. As the evening wore on, she almost convinced herself that she didn't really want a boy who preferred girls like Kathy. Almost.

Richard and she were the first ones to leave because she wanted to get up early enough to have breakfast with her mother at the airport. When they got to her house, she said, "Thanks for taking me, Richard. I had a nice time."

"I did, too," he answered.

Jeanne leaned over and kissed him on the cheek, then slid out of the car very quickly before he could react. She was smiling as she walked up to the door. Girls didn't always have to wait to be kissed, did they?

On Wednesday she called Frank Sutton

and arranged for an audition at the Old Globe for the following Friday after school. He told her she'd need a letter from her drama coach and written permission from her parents. "And don't think that all you have to do is fill out the papers," he warned. "We take almost no high school students."

"I look grown-up," she promised over the telephone. "I'm five feet nine inches tall and I wear a size-fourteen dress." Would he think she was too big to even try out? She tried to reason with herself that she wasn't really overweight anymore, but the old dreadful feelings of fatness hovered in her mind.

"Big, strong girl," Sutton laughed.

Though Jeanne knew he was teasing, her face flushed in shame. She managed to control her voice as she said, "I'll do anything. I've wanted to work at the Old Globe since I was seven years old."

"You can always volunteer to sell tickets or pass out programs," he said. Jeanne wasn't sure whether he was being sarcastic.

In a dark blue dress and her medium-heeled shoes, she looked quite grown-up, and while she didn't feel thin, she thought she would pass for normal weight. Her success of the week before gave her courage, and she tried to look very confident as she walked into the theater where Sutton and two other men waited for her.

He greeted her by name and said, "I remember you now. You've lost weight?"

"I can't remember," Jeanne admitted. "I've lost weight and gained some back." As she talked, she wished she could bite her tongue to keep silent. Frank Sutton was probably just being pleasant and she'd been so nervous that she'd as much as admitted that she had a weight problem.

"I think you were heavier," he said. "Now this is Buster Kemp and Mike Martin. We're on the hiring squad."

When Jeanne didn't laugh, he repeated his joke, "Hiring squad, that's like firing squad. That's supposed to be funny."

"I'm sorry," Jeanne said. "I guess I'm too nervous to laugh."

"You've always got to laugh at the boss's corny jokes," Frank said. "That's the first survival rule of interviews. Shall we try it again?"

"Do we have to?" She was smiling now. Maybe it would be all right trying out for him. Maybe it wouldn't be a total disaster.

"What would you like to do for us?" Frank Sutton asked.

"I'll do two parts," Jeanne said. "Juliet and the nurse."

"Not at the same time, I hope?"

"No." Jeanne laughed. "I'm pretty good but I'm not quite that good yet." She was terrified inside, but doing her best not to let Frank Sutton see it. She sensed he would be the one who really decided whether or not she was accepted, because he was the one who did all the talking. And he had once warned her to get right out there and push for success. So she tried her most dazzling, successful smile and asked, "Which do you want first?"

"Juliet."

She stepped up on the stage, took a deep breath, willed herself to look beautiful and slender, and began. " 'Oh Romeo, Romeo! wherefore art thou Romeo? / Deny thy father, and refuse thy name; / Or, if thou wilt not, be but sworn my love, / And I'll no longer be a Capulet./ ' "

As she spoke the famous lines she put her whole heart into the part. She saw herself clearly in that white satin dress, wearing that small beaded cap. She was Juliet and she knew she'd done a good job when she turned to Frank Sutton and the two other men.

Sutton didn't look very impressed as he

asked, "What else can you do?"

The lack of interest in his voice terrified her. But she was determined to show these men that she was a real actress. She took a deep breath and put her hands on her hips in a belligerent stance.

"I'll show you the nurse," she shouted and leaned forward to the empty auditorium. Then she shook her head at them and strode across the stage, putting every bit of broad comedy that she could into the part. When she recited her lines, it was with a rougher, rasping voice. She made herself believe she was in full make-up and wearing the funny costume. She did her very best to be old and ugly and as different from Juliet as she could be.

When she finished, they whispered with each other for a minute and then Frank Sutton said, "Julie, come on down here."

"Jeanne," she corrected him. "Jeanne Lee." Her heart was thumping with excitement now. If it was bad news, it would kill her. To be this close to achieving her heart's desire and not reach it would be more than she could bear.

"You say you'd like to be an apprentice here?" Buster Kemp asked her.

"Yes, sir."

"And your parents know that means long hours? No pay? Just hard work?"

"They know. And I'm a hard worker."

"We'll see," Kemp said doubtfully.

"Does that mean yes?" she directed her question to Sutton.

He nodded but he was frowning.

She ignored his expression. He'd given his approval, that was all that mattered. She said, "Thank you!"

"You may not thank us when you see what hard work means. Ever do any carpentry?" Kemp asked.

"I can learn," Jeanne said.

"How about sound equipment?" Frank Sutton asked. "Think you can learn that, too?"

"I can learn it all," Jeanne promised. "And you won't be sorry, you'll see."

"We'll see," Frank Sutton said. "Can you come in next week?"

"No," Jeanne said. "I can't come for at least three weeks. I have to finish my classes." When she saw the look on their faces she asked, "Is that too late?"

The men looked at each other and Jeanne's heart began to thump in that old familiar way. She said, "I could come in on Saturdays and Sundays. Maybe most nights. Would that help?"

"What time do you get out of school?" Kemp asked.

"Three-thirty."

"All right. Get here by four and we'll put you on the stage crew. You can help move the sets for *Darling Love*."

"And if you can move sets silently enough," Kemp said, "we might give you a walk-on part in *Midsummer Night's Dream*. How does that sound?"

"Wonderful!"

Frank Sutton walked out of the theater with her. "You have a ride?" he asked.

"My stepmother is waiting for me. Which part did you like best? Did you like my Juliet?" Jeanne couldn't resist asking.

"My dear child, your Juliet was fine, but you have too much talent to play ingenue roles. May I give you some advice?"

"Of course."

"If you really want a career in the theater, go for the meaty parts and let the others fight over the bones. You'll live longer and be happier if you concentrate on learning to act and stop worrying about being a leading lady."

"You thought I was better in the nurse's role?"

"Not particularly. I just thought it was a more amusing role."

They were at the car now and Frank Sutton leaned over and held his hand out to Amanda. He said, "Congratulations. Your stepdaughter just landed the worst job she could possibly find. Long hours and no pay. I just hope she thinks it is worth it."

"She knows what she wants," Amanda said. "Jeanne is very mature for her age."

"I hope so," the actor said. As he strode away, he turned and added over his shoulder, "See you tomorrow."

Once they were driving out of the parking lot, Amanda asked, "What's this about tomorrow? Don't they know you have to go to school?"

"I'm working after school and on weekends until school closes. I guess they need me."

"What about homework?"

"I'll manage," Jeanne said. "I'll spend lunch hour in the library and get up earlier in the morning if I need to."

Amanda shook her head. "Your father isn't going to like this."

"You can handle him," Jeanne answered, and then she laughed aloud. "If you handle Daddy, I promise you that I'll handle everything else." At that moment, she felt as though she could literally accomplish anything she wanted to.

Amanda laughed, too, and said, "It's a deal."

Chapter 17

She couldn't wait to get to drama class to tell everyone about her new job.

"Nice!" Mr. Murphy said.

Someone asked how much it paid. Jeanne laughed and said, "It doesn't pay anything. I'm just really lucky they're letting me work."

"Who would want a job like that?" Larry Spence asked.

"I would," Jeanne said crossly. She hadn't liked Larry since the day he'd teased David about being pretty enough to play Juliet. "It's a real honor to be selected. I'll be the only high school student in the program." Why was she so disappointed in their response? Why did it matter what these kids thought? She knew it was a real achievement, even if they didn't.

"What will you do?" someone else asked.

"Lots of things," Jeanne answered. "A lot of stage work, maybe some carpentry and painting."

She heard Larry's words clearly, though they were directed to the student who sat beside him. He said, "They probably picked her because of her muscles. She's built like a lady wrestler."

Jeanne bit her lip and looked at the floor until she got her breathing under control. She wanted to get up out of her chair and start pounding on Larry, but of course she wouldn't. She would simply erase him from her mind permanently. She hated herself for caring about what he said.

Mr. Murphy said, "We should all be proud that one of our members has been honored. Let's applaud ourselves and Jeanne."

Some of the class clapped politely, but their attention came too late to dissolve the pain. Jeanne sincerely wished the floor would open up and swallow her. Or maybe a nice tidal wave, Jeanne thought. No tidal wave came, and the floor stayed steady. Mr. Murphy began lecturing everyone on the importance of theater in other cultures. Jeanne sat quietly, willing herself to regain her composure, and telling herself that she'd learned a lesson.

She would never again try and share her artistic ambition with clods like Larry Spence, who couldn't appreciate anything. And she wouldn't let his cruel remark hurt her because she didn't care anything at all about him.

On the way out of class, David said, "I think it's great that you were chosen, Jeanne. Congratulations."

David smiled at her. There were a million things she would have liked to say to him, but none of them would be said. There was nothing she could say to David that would make him love her. She just smiled back. "Thanks. I'll take all the encouragement I can get."

"You'll do great," he said, before turning to look for Kathy.

She watched him walk away, wishing him well and wishing that things were different. Wishing even more that she were different. Then she sighed and muttered to herself, "No sense moping over spilt boyfriends. Better get to work."

When she reported to the theater at four, no one seemed to know who she was or to be expecting her. Finally, she went up to a man in a sweat shirt and said, "I'm supposed to be working here, so what should I do?"

"How should I know?"

"Someone should know," she insisted. "Who's in charge?"

"No one." He had a book in his hand and he opened it.

"Then how do I know what to do?"

"I guess you just pitch in," he answered. "Now, do you mind going away. I'm studying my lines."

"I *do* mind," Jeanne said. "I've had all the rejection I can handle today."

"No one has all the rejection they can stand," the young man said. "Not in the theater." He turned from her and started reading.

Jeanne stared at his back a minute and then went over to a group of three people who were painting some wooden boards. She said, "Need some help?" Then she picked up a paintbrush and joined in before they could protest.

But the second day someone spoke to her first, and on the third day, another person actually said, "Oh, here's Jeanne. Good. She can help with the boat scene."

By the end of her first week, Jeanne felt as though she'd been working at the Old Globe all of her life. As the youngest member of the crew, she got bossed around by just about everyone. She went for Cokes, mailed letters, cleaned paintbrushes, and stapled canvas.

She was surprised at how stiff she was the first few days because she was using so many new muscles. Painting flats was the hardest because you had to bend over for long periods of time without a break. She learned a lot, though, even from the simplest job she was given.

School was a lot harder than she'd expected. Studying for exams at five o'clock in the morning wasn't easy after being up till eleven or twelve the night before, and classes seemed terribly dull after the exciting time she was having at the theater. But she knew she had to keep her grades up because she had fought hard to get permission from her father for her to be in the apprentice program.

Unimpressed with her success in getting the job, her friends only complained about her lack of time for them. It hurt a little bit, but if friends didn't support you in your work, they weren't really good friends anyway, Jeanne reasoned.

Drama class was the hardest part of the day because she still felt humiliated every time she saw Larry, and because David was there. By the second week, she could look at Larry without feeling rage, but she knew she would always feel a little sad when she saw David.

On Monday of the second week, David asked her, "You coming to the class party this weekend?" At some other, younger time, she might have hoped that David was going to ask her out, but now she knew he was just making conversation.

"I'll have to work."

He nodded and sat down in preparation for another of Mr. Murphy's lectures.

Jeanne heard almost nothing of the lecture. She doodled in her notebook, jotting down the numbers of her weight. She started with the high ones, then crossed them out, going all the way down to 140 and then bouncing back up to 145. She looked a long time at that figure — 145 — and finally put a circle around it. There was no doubt about the fact that the number kept coming up in her life. Every time she ate anything at all, her weight bounced back to 145 and it was the goal weight that Anna Marie at Weight Watchers had originally picked for her.

"What are you writing?" Darla's voice startled Jeanne.

Jeanne shut the notebook quickly and said, "I didn't hear the bell ring."

"You were lost in a fog. You look sleepy," Darla said. "Want to walk home together?"

"Can't. I'm going to the theater."

"I forgot," Darla said. Then she added, "I miss you. All Kathy talks about is boys and clothes. I mean, I guess that's all I talk about, too, but you always make me laugh."

"That's me, the jolly fat lady," Jeanne said and yawned.

"You're not fat," Darla said. "Not anymore. You're big — I mean tall. But you're not fat."

"I'm not exactly thin, either. You know, I really don't eat very much anymore, but my weight won't stay down unless I starve."

"Maybe your body is trying to tell you something," Darla said."

"I think I'm listening!" Jeanne said and laughed.

During the next few days she thought a lot about her weight. Despite her grueling schedule, she'd done well on her program and she was now ready to admit that if she ate anywhere near normally, she was going to stay at 145. The only time she'd ever dipped below that was when she'd skipped three meals in a row and was faint from hunger. Then she'd been down to 142, but the next morning she popped back up to 145.

The strangest thing about her weight was that she had no trouble staying at

145 at all. All during finals week she ate healthy food because she wanted to be strong, and her weight stayed the same.

On the last day of finals, as Amanda was driving her to school, Jeanne asked, "You think I look all right now? Not too fat?"

"You look great."

"You don't think another fifteen pounds would make me beautiful?"

"No, I don't," her stepmother answered emphatically. "I think another fifteen pounds would make you look like a plucked chicken. I know that skinny is stylish, but you're not really built to be thin, Jeanne."

"I'm built like my great-aunt Mildred." Jeanne laughed. "But I try not to think about it very often."

"You've simply got to learn to accept yourself as you really are."

"By that you mean as the beautiful and talented Jeanne Lee?" Her voice was light but the question was serious.

"Yes."

"Okay. You talked me into it," Jeanne said. "From now on, I'm at my goal weight and all I have to do is stay there. And my next goal is to learn to love myself. Right?"

"Right." Amanda looked straight ahead, trying hard not to show the obvious pleasure she felt at finally winning her point.

Jeanne looked out the window of the car at the glorious sunshine and said nothing else at all. When they got to school, she leaned over and said, "Know what, Amanda?"

"What?"

"You're pretty close to perfect yourself. Now wish me luck on my chemistry final."

Amanda's eyes showed her love. "You make your own luck, Jeanne. You always will."

That afternoon in drama class, high school yearbooks were distributed. Any hope that Mr. Murphy had of teaching quickly disappeared as students raced through the pages, searching for their own pictures and those of their friends. There was a whole section on the class play, and they gathered into clumps to talk and laugh about those photos.

"Look at you, you look so silly!" Marybeth said and pointed her finger at the photograph of Jeanne in the nurse's costume. Jeanne was making a funny face and underneath the close-up was a caption that read, "Our Most Talented Actress."

Jeanne laughed automatically, but she

wasn't really looking at that photograph. It was another one that riveted her attention. Most of the photos were of the dress rehearsal and she was in that silly costume, but there was one of her in street clothes. She was standing beside Marybeth and David and two other students who were on the crew. And what fascinated her about the photograph was that she didn't look fat at all.

She stared and stared at it, reaching back in her mind to find out how much she'd weighed when that photo was taken. She was pretty sure it was the same as she weighed now — 145 pounds. Even so, she didn't look fat. Sure, she was tall and she was broad-shouldered, but she wasn't fat. She was normal-looking. In fact, she might almost be called slender, though she would never be small.

Jeanne smiled down at her face in the photograph and then traced the body with her finger. She was standing sideways and she looked fine. She was simply a trim, healthy-looking girl, not too different from the other two girls in the photo.

I'm really not fat! she thought, and the idea made her laugh. It seemed suddenly to be a big joke that she was perfectly normal in appearance.

"What's so funny?" Marybeth asked.

"Life," Jeanne said, laughing again.

Her good mood stayed with her for the rest of the evening, and every once in a while she'd start to laugh over nothing at all. That photograph had released a burden and she felt a lot lighter than she had the day before. Life *was* funny, she decided. Once she'd really seen herself, she was able to accept herself as she was.

The first performance of *Darling Love* was the Friday night that school was out, so Jeanne missed the end-of-the-school-year parties. She didn't really mind, though, because she found the theater so much more interesting. Crawling around on a stage in blackness in between scenes might not have seemed like much of a job to an outsider, but Jeanne had learned enough about how a play worked to know that a quiet scene-shifting was very important.

She invited Richard to come to the Sunday night performance of *Darling Love*. As he drove her home from the theater that night, he said, "You weren't quite as much the star as you were in the last play, but you were terrific."

"What are you talking about?" Jeanne laughed. "I hope you didn't see me moving things around."

"I didn't exactly *see* you," he teased. "But I felt your presence up there. Even in a pitch-black room in that black hood and tights you have that special something that the audience senses."

"Next month you may get to see me really," Jeanne said. "Frank says I can have a walk-on part in *Midsummer Night's Dream*."

"That's great — and you're having fun?" Richard asked.

"Yes. It's awfully hard work, but it will be easier now that school is over." Jeanne yawned and then she shook her head. "Tomorrow I'm going to spend the whole day in bed. It's my first free day in a month. And from now on I'll have every Monday off. Monday, glorious Monday."

"I was hoping we might play tennis."

"We might," Jeanne agreed. "But after noon. I want to sleep as long as possible."

"I'll pick you up at one-thirty," he said. "And maybe the next Monday we can do something more exciting. I only have one class at eight in the morning. So we could drive up to the coast. Maybe even go to the beach?"

"Sounds like fun," Jeanne said. It was nice to know that Richard wanted to spend time with her.

He kissed her good-night then, holding

her close for a minute and then saying, "I guess you know I think you're special, Jeanne."

"I know we're good friends," Jeanne said quickly.

"More than friends, I hope."

"I like you a lot, Richard." Jeanne said carefully. "And it's been a lot of fun going out with you. But you know I'm more interested in being an actress than anything in the world."

"All work and no romance makes for a very dull life," Richard said, and pulled her close to him to kiss her again.

She pulled way, laughing lightly as she said, "This is the time when I turn into a pumpkin. See you tomorrow."

"I think I'm in love with you, Jeanne."

Jeanne was startled. "What? Do you really mean that?"

"Really. Jeanne, I want to know if you . . . if you think you could love me, too."

"Richard," she began, trying to sort out her emotions. She was dismayed that the strongest one seemed to be relief. Richard had said he loved her, and she would never again need to worry that no boy would be interested in her. The second strongest emotion she felt was gratitude.

"Richard, I'm too young and I have so much going on in my life right now. . . ."

"That's part of what I love about you," he said. "You're the kind of person who will always have some excitement and fun in her life. I want to be a part of that."

"You are," she assured him. "We'll play tennis tomorow. Next week we can go to the beach. We'll have lots of fun. And we have plenty of time."

"Plenty," he echoed.

Before he could say anything else, she slipped from the car and said, "Thanks for the buggy ride."

Once inside, she poured herself a glass of milk and made a peanut butter and jelly sandwich. Then she took one bite of the sandwich and poured the milk down the sink. Slowly, deliberately, she ran the rest of the sandwich down the garbage disposal. Since she really was hungry, she took an apple out of the refrigerator and ate it, thinking about Richard, and David, and everything that had happened.

Later, when she was brushing her teeth and washing her face, she made faces at herself in the mirror and whispered sweet nothings to her reflection. "Hey, Jeanne Lee, I think I am beginning to love you, myself. You know, you're pretty okay."

She reached for the light switch. "Keep it up, Juliet," she said, and made her exit.